I0846562

Restless Crows is a collection of loosely connected short stories by Stephen Schulz (author of The Maid and Modern Fairy Tales). Described as a mixture of "magical realism" and "black comedy" by some, or "a cross between Vonnegut and Kafka" by others, Schulz breaks genres with this bizarre new anthology. An obvious theme throughout his work is the disintegration of the nuclear family in America, but it is by no means limited to such a boring and overcooked idea. Through the sorcery of his prose, Schulz launches from this basic premise and takes the reader to places no one would ever expect.

For Michael Blue, you got me through this

GEKKER PUBLISHING

Copyright © 2024 by Stephen Schulz

Published 2024 by Gekker Publishing

http://gekkerpublishing.com

Seattle, WA 98118

First Edition

Printed in the United States

Logo design by Rachel Kotkin

Cover art and all illustrations © 2024 by Rachel Kotkin

ISBN-13: 979-8-9918840-5-1

RESTLESS CROWS

-a new anthology of related stories-

by Stephen Schulz

CONTENTS

IN THE GARDEN

The crows were restless that day. They exhibited a behavior known officially as "cacophonous aggregation," usually occurring in the presence of a dead conspecific; when one or more crows gather around a fallen comrade and skold (a guttural squawk repeated in short concessions). These calls differ contextually from a simple alarm call to signal danger—the phenomenon is truly a crow funeral (of sorts), though the exact function of the behavior, and whether crows actually possess a

complex understanding of death, is unknown. (How appropriate that a "murder of crows" can also be a funeral).

The crows were restless that day. They skolded and they skolded. They had circled the house all morning; an incredible fluttering of wings, a great black mass, a ravenous, murderous funeral of crows. One of their species had eaten toxic pellets by a backyard shed with a rat problem. The pellets had been stuffed into irresistible chunks of cheese. However, it was the Bauermann's garden across the street that the crow chose as its final resting place. Its body was already decomposing due to anticoagulant chemicals that deflated the bird by way of severe bleeding. A puddle of black feathers, crow's feet, and beak sank into the soil behind a large Iris plant, never to be noticed by anyone.

Lucy Bauermann always averted her gaze in a marital argument. She retreated into a niche within, ever fortified by denying her glance to Eli. He always looked on, waiting and hopeful for that time when Lucy might raise her eyes back up to his. She would sit and he would most usually stand. Eli's standing annoyed Lucy, she felt as if he was looming over her. Eli did not think that he loomed. He was standing then, when there was a knock at the door. Lucy stared into the void from her seat and Eli walked over to answer. It was usually expected of him to answer the door.

Eli first peeked through the narrow window on the door to see who it was. He did not recognize the man, dressed in overalls and looking out over the garden with an odd smirk. The man caressed the stubble on his chin with a charade of pensiveness.

"Hello?" said Eli.

The man took his time to acknowledge Eli's presence. He slowly turned his head and shifted his line of sight from the garden to Eli. His smirk became larger, a forced smile that was painful to perform. His hand remained on his chin. He spoke through his teeth with an accent Eli could not place.

"Hi, I was hoping to get flowers," the man said.

"Flowers?"

"I was driving, my truck is there, and I see your flowers." He brought both his hands up to frame a tall row of old lilacs, blooming with the full glory of spring. The fragrance from the flowers was so pungent it nearly made the air shimmer. An open window wafted the scent indoors from night to early morning, filling the living room with a sweet perfume.

"Oh, you'd like to take home some lilac flowers. Yes, by all means, take a few."

"I have a tool in my truck and I'd like to cut some branches with the flowers."

"Sure, OK, cut a branch, just please don't leave the tree in an awkward shape."

"Yes, I'd like to cut some branches."

"Well, how many branches are we talking here?"

"Well, we need flowers for the weekend and I see your flowers and I love them."

"Surprising somebody?"

"No, we have an event, we need flowers."

"How many flowers do you need?"

"How many flowers will you let me have?"

"Oh, I don't know, a dozen small branches, at the top where it could use some pruning, I noticed you have a ladder on your truck."

"Just a dozen?"

"Yes, well, we like to look at them, but I suppose I could spare a dozen."

"I'll get my tool." The man went across the street to where his pickup was parked. He pulled from the back a long tool nearly two meters in length with a curved saw blade on the end of it. Just beneath the saw was a lopper connected to a draw string that activated it, running the length of the pole-handle.

Eli went back inside the house. Lucy was still looking at the floor. Eli peered out from behind a curtain which partially covered an open window by the lilacs. The man with the pruner impressed Eli with his swift skill, adroitly removing each carefully selected branch in a sharp instant.

"He looks like a professional," Eli said. Lucy said nothing. Eli then finally registered the racket he had heard all morning as an enormous congregation of crows. He wanted to make a comment but knew it would anger Lucy as it was a frivolous distraction from their argument. He should be reengaging with her, he thought, but the man outside seemed done. Eli hurried back out the door.

"You all done?" said Eli.

"Ah, yes," said the man. He adjusted his hat and a bead of sweat rolled down his face.

"Great, wow, you work fast, and the pruning actually looks nice that way."

"Yeah, you know, I really would like to get those guys up there," the man pointed to a couple of high branches that were loaded with plump clusters of purple flowers. He shrugged his shoulders. "But I already have a dozen."

"Well go ahead and get those two at the top, that's fine."

The man extended his device, pulling out a pole that had fit snugly into the pole-handle, doubling the length of the reach. Eli did not go back inside. He stood on the front porch and watched the man for a moment.

"So this event on the weekend, is it a wedding or a birthday?"

"Oh, no-no-no, it's at the market, the farmers' market."

"The farmers' market, OK, so some social event at the market?"

"No." The man cut the last of the two branches. "We are selling flowers at the market—I would like to get that guy too, but," the man shrugged as he did before, "that's OK I guess," he shook his head gently and let out a tisk-tisk from between his teeth.

"Alright, well, good luck selling my flowers at the market."

"Yes, I'll get this stuff together here, and I'll go, OK?"

"Sounds good, thanks, good luck." Eli watched the man gather his cuttings and tool into one mass that he then expertly hoisted over his shoulder and carried to the bed of his truck. Eli waved as the man looked over while climbing into the driver's seat. The man gave a limp wave in return and shut the door to his vehicle. Eli went back inside. He knew he should continue his conversation with Lucy, and that he had welcomed the interruptions, but he still needed to tend to the garden and chicken coop before it got too late and too hot outside.

"He's gone," said Eli. Lucy raised her eyebrows and gave a slight nod while looking down at her mobile phone, her thumbs typing on the screen with strong intent. "I have to go and take care of the chickens, and I should water, it's supposed to be a scorcher today... I'll be right back." There was a pause. "Did you hear that?"

"Yeah, OK," said Lucy.

The Bauermanns could not afford to install an irrigation system, that is why Eli always watered by hand with a hose. He was able, however, to attach an inexpensive brass nozzle to the end of the hose that, when loosened, would let out a pressurized stream of water. When tightened, the fixture would gradually lose its forceful propulsion and transform the emission into a fine mist before shutting off altogether.

Eli took a moment to close his eyes and breathe the sweet inchoate air of early morning. Then, upon raising his eyelids, he noticed the house across the street. It had been occupied until the week before but now it appeared empty. He saw the darkness past the front door, slightly ajar, still and deep in the stagnant morning sunlight, and it mysteriously nauseated him. The neighbors who had lived there (for about a year) he had never spoken to beyond a few passing banalities at the mailboxes. And yet, he had a keen awareness of their presence: they were an ageless couple who fought constantly. Their yells echoed down the residential block almost daily. During their more heated bouts, Eli would tip-toe into the front garden giggling to himself and hide behind a tree, attempting to eavesdrop like an old gossip. But alas, their high-energy, high-decibel arguments were devoid of any true intelligibility, so Eli was never able to actually comprehend what their altercations were about. Nonetheless, he found their tangled vocal tangos amusing.

Eli turned the nozzle to let water out of the hose and forgot about the sick feeling. Practicing his watering technique seemed always to help him feel more at ease. Eli had become quite adept at using the hose apparatus to suit the dynamic needs of watering the garden: he swiftly adjusted the nozzle from a gentle spray over the peonies to a hard jet to attack a wasps' nest; he shifted in an instant from the droplets that mimicked a light rain on the raspberries to a conical emission that expertly soaked a ring of green beans growing up their poles.

With watering finished, Eli's next duty was to attend to the backyard chicken coop. He walked into the sunroom at the back of their house and filled a pitcher of feed from the sack he kept there. He remembered then that he left some table scraps as a treat for the chickens in a tub by the kitchen sink, but he did not want to go back inside. He took the food that he had and opened the wire door to the pen. He filled a feeder that he had constructed out of milk jugs and suspended from a cord of nylon nailed to the ceiling of the enclosure. The chickens swarmed the feeder in a frenzy. Midst the frantic beaks, one of the lower ranking individuals pecked at some feed that landed on his shoe, surprising him.

Eli saw that the water dispenser was low and filthy. He removed it and cleaned the crud with a sharp stream from the brass nozzle before filling it again with water. By the time Eli placed the water in the pen the chickens had mostly lost their interest in feeding and began to venture out of the pen to graze in the backyard. It was then that Eli noticed the presence of only five of the six chickens. Joan was missing.

Joan was Eli's favorite chicken and the alpha of the pecking order. On windy days it was Joan's habit to stand apart from the rest of the flock at the edge of the garden, staring through the chain-link fence while the wind ruffled her beautiful barred rock feathers. Eli would joke that Joan was like a true leader, gazing into the future.

Eli opened the door to the coop to check on Joan. The cool temperature of morning was quickly disappearing and the inside of the coop already felt hot and stifled. There was also a peculiar humidity to the air that made Eli imagine the inside of a blister. Joan was perched in the same spot where Eli had left her the previous evening—he had seen Joan sitting on the ground of the coop that night, thought she had been confused by the dark, and so placed her on the long wooden perch with the others. She had not moved since. Gently, Eli placed a hand over each wing to carry Joan into the outside light for inspection. On the underside of the chicken, Eli touched a cool neglectful liquid that slipped along the fissures of his calloused fingertips and poured into the pores of his skin with an almost preternatural potency, the effect of which was unknown to him. Stepping into the sunlight, Eli looked the bird in the eye—she was vacant and listless. Superficially, he investigated the feathers around her neck and wings, yet he knew the problem was underneath.

Finally, Eli flipped the chicken over. Though there was a strong visual, what struck him first was the odor—it was not that he had not smelled the odor prior to looking, he had catalogued in his automatic mind an oddly unpleasant scent, but it did not hit him fully and consciously until he was faced with it: a glistening scent of decay that blurred the air immediately near to it. Then, a moment later, after Eli's eyes adjusted to the sizzling putrid atmosphere, he saw what watery tickle had caressed his hands: a myriad of maggots writhing in a fetid soiree. The maggots had apparently made their home in a slash-like wound that ran the length of the bird's underside, and expanded into an inexplicable maze of skin folds and dark dripping feathers. At the center of it all was a large bubble of exposed grey-damp skin.

Eli began to choke on the atmosphere. There was a dangerous filth to the air that twisted in his nostrils. His eyes began to water, or perhaps it was that he wept, Eli could not tell the difference. He had on him a pocket knife that he unfolded in a desperate attempt to lance the pustule on the poor bird. He peeled some more of the feathers around the boil to clear an area—the soaked feathers detached from the surface of the hen like clumps of warm butter. Steadily he held his small blade and punctured the balloon of grey skin which deflated rapidly, oozing a surprisingly clear fluid. He then pulled the knife across the loose skin, creating a long slit with relative ease. Eli pinched the top flap of skin and tore it to expose the flesh beneath—not raw but rather greenish, a deeper decay. Eli tore at the skin still further beyond where the pustule had been. The denizens of the rot seemed almost aggravated by this action which gave Eli some hope that he may rid Joan of them. He gave what little skin he could hold between the tips of his fingers a confident tug and ripped away a gelatinous triangle. But then Eli gasped—revealed were many layers, nonsensical layers, all teaming with maggots. He knew then that it was hopeless.

"I'm so sorry Joan, I'm so sorry. This is it, poor girl, this is it," Eli spoke to the chicken, who had remained motionless through the surgery.

Eli stood. Joan stayed on her side, too weak to even attempt to change position. Eli made his way to the shed not far from where Joan lay, the shed where he kept his tools. Inside there was what he needed: a hatchet he rarely used. He also looked for a board of some kind to place under Joan, so that he may strike against a hard surface and give her a quick death. Leaned up against the wall was a pile of sticks used as stakes for gardening and behind them was a flat board of wood, about 20 centimeters wide and one and a half meters in length. It was perfect for the job.

Softly, Eli laid Joan onto the board. She stretched her legs in a way that Eli interpreted to be an invitation, as if she had a secret knowledge of what was to come. Eli thought that he should cause her no panic and so covered her eyes with his palm. He aimed the small axe and rehearsed the motion, steadying his nerves. He then raised the hatchet to the appropriate distance, held his breath in concentration and brought it down swiftly. The head came off in a clean instant and Eli commended himself on his accuracy. Eli expected (according to common knowledge, having had no previous experience) the body of the chicken to scurry about wildly, but it was instead that the bird only slightly jerked its body in a pathetic weak manner. Eli removed his hand from Joan's face and watched her softly close her eyes—he thought this meant she was relieved.

Eli took the spade he kept against the coop, sheltered by a bit of awning. The shovel had seemed to Eli to lean morosely against the old wood of the coop exterior. There was then the question of where to dig. Eli noticed a small patch of dirt behind some phlox in a fenced-off flower bed the chickens were kept from grazing in. Joan would have wanted to get in there and explore, Eli thought, and so he began to dig.

Eli was surprised at how large the hole needed to be—he placed Joan's body in the initial hole he had dug and it did not appear to adequately fit. He dug it wider and deeper to accommodate the bird's bulk. He was then about to cover the corpse when he realized that he had forgotten Joan's head. He was much gentler with the head and cradled it in his hands as if it were fragile and precious. He placed the head down on the ground a moment so that he may turn the rotten side of the body away and lay the head upon her cushiony feathers, as beautiful as they ever were. Upon doing so, Eli felt an odd sort of misery, one that was sick and hazy. It was unfamiliar to him and yet also known, as if having welcomed something strange but inexorable.

Eli covered the sad bits of chicken offal (that unfathomably Joan was once comprised of) with earth, though he thought that perhaps it was not enough. He felt he needed a marker to commemorate Joan, as he had had no sepulcher to house her corpse.

It was convenient, however, that many months prior, while trimming roses along a fence, Eli had found an old bowling ball hidden among some dead intertwined stems. Remembering this bowling ball, Eli thought that it would make a suitable tombstone. As Eli pulled the bowling ball out from under the roses, and schlepped it across the lawn, he noticed that it was much heavier than he imagined, almost unbearably heavy. He set it in the dirt over Joan. Eli coughed and told himself he hoped he was not coming down with a cold, though in reality he had simply fought back tears.

Eli returned indoors. The salient features of his presence, as detected by Lucy, were his outstretched arms and rigid hands, palms down, accompanied by an abnormal gait. She understood this behavior to be a theatrical display of hardships which had kept him outside for a prolonged duration of time. However, Lucy did not buy it, she saw through his spurious antics and attributed the delay to his usual desultory dillydallying. The strange mummy-like gesticulation of his arms and hands she execrated to be nothing more than the product of the rhapsodic intensity he experienced whilst practicing his hobby—alone and safe without the "nagging wife." She wondered if he really thought she was as horrid as that. Lucy considered Eli's silent judgment of her character to be wholly unfair, even cruel.

Eli awkwardly and desperately washed his hands in the kitchen sink. He spoke across the house to the living room where Lucy still sat and told her of the incident matter-of-factly. Lucy, though never a true caretaker of the chickens, expressed not only shock but an almost loving sort of grief as to the loss of Joan. She had a subtle sob at the back of her throat as she spoke. Her expressed concern provided Eli with a sense of intimacy that he had long forgotten about. He warmed to Lucy within himself and capitulated to admitting whatever wrong he had committed (so he might become, once again, physically close in addition to the emotional intimacy that she had so poignantly resurrected in him). Then he noticed the smell. Eli realized that merely washing his hands was not helping the rot that aggressively invaded his nose. Lucy too quickly became aware of the foul odor and voiced her complaint. Eli decided to shower, and to launder his clothing, which Lucy concurred as the right course of action.

A week to the day after Joan's death, the Bauermanns' television broke. Joan was not consequential to the machine breaking but it was noted nevertheless by the Bauermanns as a "sign." A few days later a large package was dropped at their front door. They were not expecting a parcel of any kind, least of all a monolithic package that stood triumphantly on their front porch. To their surprise and joy, however, the Bauermanns soon found that in the mysteriously giant box was an enormous television. Lucy's father had bought for them the television as an act of sheer kindness (knowing via a phone conversation that they had recently become television-less). It was much larger than their old television and not the sort they would normally be able to afford. There was only one problem: it did not fit on the old stand and they did not have anything else to put it on.

Eli went to the tool shed to look for a possible solution—there, in a sad dark corner, was the board he had used when euthanizing Joan. It was the perfect length and width for the legs of the television. He grabbed the board and placed it so that either end stretched equally beyond the edges of the old stand. The legs of the new television set fit perfectly on the board. A simple tablecloth hid the tacky appearance of the naked wood jutting beyond the edges of the old stand, proportionate though it was.

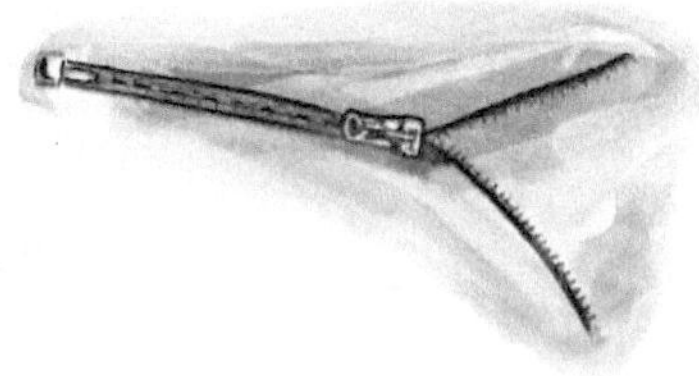

TO CATCH A TRAIN

The crows were restless that day. They exhibited a behavior known officially as "cacophonous aggregation," usually occurring in the presence of a dead conspecific; when one or more crows gather around a fallen comrade and skold (a guttural squawk repeated in short concessions). These calls differ contextually from a simple alarm call to signal danger—the phenomenon is truly a crow funeral (of sorts), though the exact function of the behavior, and whether crows actually possess a complex understanding of death, is unknown. (How appropriate that a "murder of crows" can also be a funeral).

The crows were restless that day. They skolded and they skolded. They had circled the house all morning; an incredible fluttering of wings, a great black mass, a ravenous, murderous funeral of crows. One of their species had hit the bedroom window and fallen dead into the garden, a neglected tangle of weeds soldiered by vociferous wasps. The bang against the glass had woken up Franz but he was too tired to investigate, he turned and waited for his alarm. The noise did not wake Ingrid, nor did she rise when Franz's alarm did finally buzz and shriek at 8 AM. She continued to breathe softly and snore. Her snores that morning were gentle and reminded Franz of a little bird rustling in the leaves beneath a tree. Franz and Ingrid were married.

Franz sat up and rubbed his eyes as he pictured the little bird. He felt a peculiar type of weariness, one that swelled within him like a rushing tide and drowned any sense of rest. He could not fight it, there was no abating this wave of fatigue, he could only carry it like a heavy jug of water. He lifted the jug and trudged mechanically to the washroom. His hands caught the edge of the sink to prop up his body. His breath became short. It would take more than a simple rinse of the face on this day, he thought.

Franz then stepped into the shower. The water offered no refreshment but rather seemed to weigh down his limbs like an oversaturated plant that topples into the mud. Franz lacked the energy to scrub himself clean as he should, after skipping the shower the previous night. Franz could only let the shower stream down onto his shoulders. He dropped his head to face the floor as the water cascaded from his chin. His eyes were closed.

Franz dried his body before the steam-clouded mirror above the sink. He realized that he had no memory of how he arrived at the mirror from the shower, his movements had been purely automatic. Franz reached over the sink to wipe some fog from the mirror, so he could see himself. But he stopped after clearing a tiny area—he did not wish to see himself. Only his right eye was reflected, looking back at him. He noticed the fatigue in this eye. He sighed and touched his face. The roughness of his stubble dug into his soggy fingertips. He would leave it for today. He would only comb his hair. He used a small travel-sized comb—all other brushes and combs of normal size had been unconsciously confiscated for Ingrid's use.

At first the fine teeth of the little comb ran through Franz's thick black hair with relative ease. Out of routine, Franz passed the comb over the sides of his head, combed the top of his reasonably short haircut from the side part, and then finally came to the back. It was at the back of the head where Franz felt an unusual snag on the comb. Some of the plastic teeth broke and fell into the sink. An odd soreness ached where the comb had been caught. He attempted a second time and again the comb was halted in its path, producing some pain. He pulled gently down on the comb and the pain increased beyond the strange discomfort, throbbing and pulsating down his spine. Franz immediately released the pressure on the comb and the pain slowly subsided.

Franz decided he would investigate. He rummaged clumsily through Ingrid's makeup bag and found a small hand-held mirror. He cleared away the remaining condensation on the mirror above the sink, turned his back to the sink, and held up the pocket mirror. At first, it was difficult for Franz to see anything in the little mirror, since his hand trembled so. He took in a deep breath and held it for a moment. With his nerves somewhat steadied, he was then able to observe the region where the pain had come from: a translucent viscous gel clumped around the spot. Franz timidly parted the sticky hairs and saw a silver glinting object on his scalp. He leaned forward to get a better view but in effect made it more difficult to see. He corrected himself and kept the pocket mirror close to his face as he bent backwards to zoom in on the shiny material. He squinted his eyes and focused: it appeared to be a small but brightly chromed slider of a zipper, about the same length of a dime's diameter.

Franz was dumbfounded as to how a small slider of a zipper could have become stuck in his hair. Perhaps it fell off one of his wife's purses, he thought. There was also the question as to why tugging on the slider hurt so badly; perhaps there was a nerve under the skin there, he thought. Filled with new-found confidence upon likely solving the riddle, he became determined to remove the irritant. It was clear that the slider was close to his scalp, so he planned on sniping the hair just beneath it and thus needed a thin instrument. He found a small pair of scissors (belonging to Ingrid) that were perfect for the job and resumed the position from where he could view the slider. Franz prodded at it and felt a twinge, much like picking at a scab. He tried to wedge the blades of the scissors below the slider but could not seem to make any progress, and the harder he pressed the more it hurt. He leaned further back for a closer look. That was when Franz noticed, just above the slider, a pair of zipper teeth.

Franz shuddered and dropped the scissors. Outside, the wind rattled against the washroom window. Ingrid's snores erupted into explosive gusts that perfectly punctuated the wind-swept world. Franz gently felt the teeth of the zipper rub against his fingertips, almost like a nibble. The thought arose to see a doctor, but he was running late. The obvious course of action was to go to work and make an appointment while on his lunch break, hopefully for the very next day. His doctor was good about seeing him on short notice, he thought, though he had never truly seen his doctor on short notice. He wrapped a towel around himself and walked to the front door. He kept his satchel on a stool near the door. Inside his bag was his planner and so he wrote in it: "lunch- call dr."

The best thing to do in a situation like this, he thought, was to put the matter completely out of his mind until the very moment in which he had to deal with the little problem directly, beginning at lunchtime. Franz exhaled as if a weight had been lifted. He walked briskly, almost gleefully, to the laundry room where it was Franz's ritual to dress. He always laid out an outfit on top of the washing machine the night before. Franz would sometimes dry his socks and underwear for a few minutes on chilly mornings for the extra warmth.

There was a mirror in the laundry room Franz would dress by. He stood with excellent posture before this mirror and fastidiously fastened the buttons on his shirt. He did so slowly, keenly aware, and with such aplomb that for a moment he forgot all about the zipper. He felt normal. Franz unbunched his socks, as he always did, and placed them in the dryer. The weather that morning was mild, one could even say warm, but Franz clung to the security of the extra warmth, coupled with banal routine. The socks tumbled for a full five minutes while he leaned with his palms against the dryer, looking down at the glass door to the dryer cabin. He watched the inside of the contraption spin and it filled his mind with nothing, not even lint.

The machine beeped and the timed dry was over. Franz bent down to retrieve his socks. In doing so he grazed the back of his head against the top of the entry to the dryer, thus reminding him of the zipper and its strange tenderness. That mysterious organ within him sank, the one that always sank whenever he was disappointed and then rose again with time, unnoticed. Franz put on his socks and then stood to check how the entire assemblage of his garments appeared in the mirror, socks included. He saw his organ sunken face and the temptation suddenly struck him: the desire to pull at the zipper once more.

Franz crept the tips of his fingers tentatively up the back of his neck and head. His hair, still slightly wet, felt like a soft meadow damp with dew. There issued out from his scalp a seductive sensuality, as if he lay in this meadow and bathed in its moisture. His eyes closed as his index finger touched the viscous fluid that leaked from the zipper, a dripping sensual seduction of goo. And right above it was the slider, cool and rigid. He pinched the slider between his index finger and thumb and slowly pulled downward. There was pain again but it was different, a different sort of tenderness, like that of sore muscles kneaded by sympathetic hands.

The slider passed along the zipper teeth without resistance, though Franz moved the slider below each pair of teeth slowly, methodically, and with a bewildering pleasure that at the same time ran parallel to mounting apprehension. He had shifted the slider down ten pairs of teeth with gentle ease but then, abruptly, he stopped. He was afraid of how much farther it could go. And yet, Franz's fear was soon replaced with an overwhelming instinct to take his index finger and probe the space between the exposed zipper teeth.

The viscous goo fell in a clump over the back of his hand. The teeth bit down on either side of his finger as he ran it halfway up the exposed area. His eyes remaining closed, Franz applied a small amount of pressure to this space. A sizzle of tiny bubbles tickled his fingertip. He increased the pressure and pushed, so that his finger poked beyond the teeth down to the first knuckle. The effervescence rose in intensity, fizzing frenziedly around his finger. Though there was an ethereal nature to these bubbles—light, almost giddy.

Franz recoiled his finger in alarm. Nothing had happened that would have caused him to sense alarm, but that was the point: he did not know where the bizarrely pleasurable allure could take him. He feared that the cranial champagne sparkling around his finger was in some way representative of a quiet before the storm. He rubbed his index finger and thumb together. A sticky residue of the viscous fluid was dried by the friction and became coarse, flaking into tiny fragments that fell to the floor as dust. He noticed the time on his watch, which he had placed on top of the washing machine—he was running late.

Suddenly it occurred to Franz that he should not leave the zipper exposed. He quickly yanked the slider upwards and ignored the burning sensation that it caused. But it was not good enough, he must conceal the zipper altogether. He remembered an old hat that hung on a coat rack by the front door. It was a gift from an in-law bought on vacation. He rarely wore hats, and never to work, but he must, it was the only thing he could do in such a limited time frame. Still in his socks, he ran to the front door with his eyes on the slick hardwood floor along the way, then looked up. For a moment, he was startled—during the nanoseconds his brain took to properly catalogue the visual stimuli, he saw the coat rack as a bulging dark presence, skulking and grotesque. Franz nervously seized the hat, a summer straw beach hat entirely inappropriate for the rest of his dress.

As soon as he placed the straw hat on his head, an inexplicable dejection came up inside him, an emptiness in his gut. Franz labeled the feeling as hunger, he had skipped breakfast. He went to look at his watch but he had left it on the washing machine and there was not enough time to go back for it. He held onto his hat so that it would not blow away and, shutting the door behind him, immediately broke into a run. If he ran he could still catch his train, he thought.

HOMUNCULUS

The crows were restless that day. They exhibited a behavior known officially as "cacophonous aggregation," usually occurring in the presence of a dead conspecific; when one or more crows gather around a fallen comrade and skold (a guttural squawk repeated in short concessions). These calls differ contextually from a simple alarm call to signal danger—the phenomenon is truly a crow funeral (of sorts), though the exact function of the behavior, and whether crows actually possess a

complex understanding of death, is unknown. (How appropriate that a "murder of crows" can also be a funeral).

The crows were restless that day. They skolded and they skolded. They had circled the brick building since dawn; an incredible fluttering of wings, a great black mass, a ravenous, murderous funeral of crows. One of their species had become ensnared by a wad of discarded mesh, inexplicably attached to the metal frame of a fire escape. Unable to free itself from this tangled web of refuse, the creature had starved to death. Or perhaps it simply gave up living. The brick building was dirtied with the exhaust of passing trucks.

Just a couple floors above was the Kleins' apartment. The skolds woke Edith. She lay for a moment in a dreary state, at first not recognizing the skolds as bird sound. Rather, she heard an auditory undulation above the traffic din that made her feel ineffably alone. Simon did not wake. Simon dreamed. Edith did not like that Simon left her alone as he dreamed, wrapped in blankets like a warm nest, embracing a soft yielding pillow. That Simon was dreaming seemed to Edith like a betrayal and she resented the smugness of his comfort. She shook Simon and he was startled into wakefulness. Simon made loud unintelligible utterances of distress which irritated Edith.

Simon could not remember his wonderful dream. Though he tried, he could not even recall a vague impression. Edith did not care about what either she or he had dreamt. She scoffed and rushed to get ready for the day. She had many important things to do. Simon also had matters of consequence to tend to, or so he thought, and this annoyed Edith. He had no understanding, she thought. He did not know how attentively she lived by the minute, by each grain of sand in the hourglass. He had no concept of balancing the world on a pin each day, vulnerable and ready to topple. Edith skipped breakfast and left in a huff before Simon had finished getting ready. Simon would probably forget the lunch they had planned together, she thought.

Simon did not remember lunch. Edith was going to call him but she quit mid-dial. During his lunch hour, Simon got sidetracked by the mesmerizing view of the harbor downtown, glistening between the towering buildings. The gulls yelped soothing sweet nothings into the air as the sun bounced off skyscraper-glass to warm his face. He sat on a bench and ate a falafel sandwich from a food truck. Something echoed his dream but he was not quite sure what it was—it remained seductively obscure and tenuous. And yet, he knew it had something to do with the harbor. Maybe if he got closer to the water?

Simon walked down the steep blocks to the waterfront. Nothing. Soon he had to return to work, and so the strange idea came to him of collecting some sea water to bring home, perhaps in his tzatziki sauce container. Maybe something about the water itself could later jog his memory? This was nonsense, he thought, but why not? He then abandoned the idea.

Shortly before his work day was over, Simon realized that he had forgotten his lunch with Edith. He phoned Edith but she did not answer, which made him especially nervous about returning home. Normally, Simon would capitulate to this sensation of an impending confrontation, or what he called (to himself) "facing the music." However, this time was different. This time, Simon was struck by an urge to temporarily ignore and delay "facing the music." As soon as he stepped onto his commuter bus, he lunged back out again, nearly getting caught between the doors as they clanged shut. It was a decision that sprang from his body rather than his conscious mind. Surprised by himself, he thought "oh well, there's another bus in just a half hour." He then noticed, once again, the waterfront with its attractive glow. He ran down to catch the golden light of late summer shimmering in the sound. Along the pier, the happy people of the sun sauntered above a tranquil fairy-green sea. Simon savored these precious minutes by himself. He closed his eyes to the bright sun and basked in the orange nothingness that illumined his lids. But then, upon opening his eyes, he saw an empty extra-large Styrofoam cup in a garbage bin, and that strange idea from lunch returned.

Edith prepared dinner at home. She sliced an onion and wept. She had rehearsed her confronting words to Simon while chopping vegetables. But with the sting of the onion, her internal monologue ceased. She gave up. She became unsure as to whether

her tears were genuine or caused by the onion. But she accepted these tears, nevertheless, as her own.

When Simon came home he made banal attempts at conversation, skirting the issue, though hoping Edith would bring up the offense on her own. Edith noticed a big dirty disposable cup placed on a windowsill (likely while her back was turned) but she did not bother to ask. She hardly cared. She gave Simon little in talk. As the evening went on, Simon increased his level of trite cheery engagement, without reciprocity from Edith. She remained suspended in emotional limbo. She was waiting, waiting for Simon to say the right thing (though she was unsure as to what that was, or if it would even make a difference, yet she yearned for him to try).

Simon and Edith went to bed. Edith turned her back to Simon. He let out a deep breath and felt it was time to come clean.

"I'm sorry I forgot we were going to meet for lunch. Did you wait very long in the lobby or did you just go? I woke up in such a hurry, I forgot we were going to take our breaks together," Simon said. There was silence from Edith. "I'm sorry, I was tired and dazed."

"Wow, I can't believe you waited this long to say something," Edith said, though she knew he would wait a good while to say anything.

The conversation that followed is not important—not to them nor to anyone. The Kleins went through their usual motions of conflict, repeating the same phrases that had been said for years, and progressing along a predictable pattern. Edith knew the difference between a temporary truce and genuine resolve. She made little pretense when their argument came to its inevitable conclusion, acting her role only as much as necessary (or perhaps slightly less) to get their process over with. Simon took up the slack on enthusiasm and gave a convincing performance, as if all that had been said was a revelation, as if he believed in change. Yet, in his heart Simon was just as hardened as Edith, it was merely required of him to out-perform her if they were to stay married, and this falsehood injured him greatly.

Simon did not really dream that night but woke abruptly, gasping for air. He had been doing that a lot recently and was not sure why, perhaps because he fell asleep on his back, he thought. He also attributed this breathless startle to the stuffy atmosphere now common to their bedroom (evenings were becoming chilly again so Edith used a space heater by the bed, though insisted the window be completely shut). There were still several hours before his alarm but Simon felt wide awake, and he could not stand the lack of oxygen in the room. He sought refuge in the coolness of the kitchen, where he could open a window and breathe.

There he remembered the cup on the windowsill. The surface of the polluted saltwater in the cup reflected an eerie harvest moon, which in turn was mirrored by the window. The produced effect was a mystical greenish hue that flickered before Simon's groggy gaze. A deep sense of apprehension came over him and he did not know exactly why, only that it had something to do with his dream from the previous night. He was then unsure as to whether he should open the kitchen window, for it would cause him to view the contents of the cup, and that he shuddered to think of. But then, craving the fresh air, Simon consoled himself that this behavior of his was in fact ridiculous; that this silly engagement had "gone on long enough." He should simply open the window, take the cup, dump the foul harbor water into the sink, and throw the garbage away, he thought. What had possessed him to not only capture disgusting sea water (soiled with urban runoff, boat-engine oil, and kept in a piece of trash, no less), but then to carry it home, was beyond him. He felt as if a ludicrous spell had been lifted from him. Simon quickly composed himself and walked sternly to the window, opened it, inhaled a gulp of the cool night's atmosphere, and then unceremoniously took the shabby receptacle and flung its shameful contents into the kitchen sink nearby.

What fell into the sink did not splash or splatter like water, or even like dirty water. There was instead a squishy thud that reminded Simon of when he had dropped an uncooked chicken—a slimy rubbery meat that had slipped from its tight packaging and yet was cushioned by its corpse-liquid as it plopped. The sound took the breath out of Simon, out of the entire apartment; a suspended moment of stuffy stillness. Then a tiny, faint, and pathetic cough could be heard, coming from the sink. The little cough struggled but gained in momentum and quickly morphed into a wailing cry, like that of an infant.

Simon rushed to the sink in a jolting, hesitant manner. He was filled both with terror over this unknown presence *and* the dread of his wife waking to witness what monstrosity he had brought into their home. What he saw, lying in a fetal position, was a miniscule human, a male, covered in a greenish, gelatinous goop. Simon thought—could it be a child? He dared not touch the creature but by some obtuse impulse he picked it up and cradled it in his hands. At once it stopped crying and began to nuzzle in the creases between Simon's fingers, eyes closed, seemingly secure. It did not appear as a baby, rather, it had an adult form, like a homunculus. Could it be, Simon thought, that this thing looks like himself?

Surely not, was Simon's answer. Granted, the homunculus had Simon's lean figure, his thick brown hair (disheveled, wavy, neither long nor short), his large eyebrows, his delicate chin and jawline. But Simon's nose bent slightly to the left, whereas the homunculus' nose was perfectly straight, nor did it possess the pointedness of Simon's ears, nor the exact wrinkles of Simon's forehead. The homunculus then began to shiver as a cool breeze from the open window caressed its moistened, naked body. It coughed, punctuated by convulsing jerks.

And then, by some mysterious caprice, Simon wept. He felt deeply for this creature; by some unknowing yet palpable force they were connected, and only now did Simon feel it. He no longer had any fear, he concerned himself only with helping the poor thing. Simon quickly shuffled through a kitchen drawer and found a couple of dish towels—one to dry the homunculus, the other to wrap him and provide warmth. The puny humanoid remained mostly still as Simon dried it, its eyes closed, and brows furrowed. Simon then adorned the creature with the remaining towel and carried it into the spare bedroom of the apartment, where Simon could investigate further without waking Edith. This extra room had been converted into a study with a desk they rarely used, and a twin mattress for overnight visitors.

Simon placed the little thing prostrate on the bed and sat by it. A moment later, it opened its eyes—gleaming with wakeful consciousness, one might even say intelligence. Simon was relieved that the thing's eyes were dark brown, while his own eyes were of a lighter shade of brown. It then opened its mouth, almost as wide as it could, and attempted what Simon thought was the first syllable of a word—a groaning, hoarse "aaahh," as if Simon was a doctor inspecting its tonsils. This groan, at first sustained, soon morphed into sudden outbursts repeated with gaining intensity. Simon was stunned, immobilized, his breath held, until finally he exhaled with a loud shushing sound. This "shhh" quieted the creature. It then looked at Simon with a knitted brow and pointed with its finger. Simon looked: it was a cup of water on the desk. He brought it to the homunculus and tilted the water to reach its wee lips. Simon expected the creature to take small sips from the rim of the cup but instead it licked the water like a cat. It drank for quite some time and Simon's wrist tired. (Each time the little thing paused and took in a breath Simon thought it was done, but before he could relax it began slurping with its tongue once more). Finally, its thirst was quenched. It sat up and again pointed: the chess set.

It had been years since Simon had played, though he was once rather good and enjoyed the game's mental exercise. Simon's set was an old wooden travel-set that folded to house the pieces inside. Simon quickly opened it up and began placing the chess pieces in their starting positions. The homunculus looked on in earnest.

"Would you like black or white?" Simon said. The miniature humanlike thing raised its eyebrows as if puzzled.

"White goes first, would you like to go first?" A long pause, absolutely vacuous, containing nothing.

"OK, I'll just make the first move," Simon said. He advanced the pawn in front of his king by two spaces. The homunculus looked at Simon quizzically.

"It's a classic opening," Simon said. The homunculus then clasped a diminutive hand around the pawn in front of his right bishop, lifted it up, and stopped. Simon nodded in such a way as to encourage movement.

"Go on, you almost have it," Simon said. The creature then held the pawn so that it hovered over the board. His eyebrows crumpled, looking severely pensive.

"That's it, you're nearly there!"

The little thing brought the chess piece, huge in its hand, to its mouth, placed its lips on the corner of it and began to blow a raspberry. It then looked at Simon with bright proud eyes, as if it had accomplished something and so sought praise. A faint smile was forming, hardly visible in the corners of its mouth. Simon took a deep breath and waited a moment.

"No, not like that," Simon said. The little thing appeared sad.

"Try again," Simon said.

The homunculus brought the pawn down onto the board with a tentative uncoordinated motion that ended with a thump. The piece wobbled a little but settled in its spot, with two spaces open between it and the bishop.

"Very good," Simon said. "A classic response to a classic opening maneuver, that's called the 'Sicilian Defense.'" The game was then cut short, Edith was stirring into wakefulness and the sun had fully emerged. Simon frantically wrote a brief excuse for Edith on a scrap piece of paper, threw on his clothes from yesterday (still on the study floor), and left with the homunculus under his coat.

Down the block was a pet store, and Simon intended to get some supplies for his new little humanoid friend. He also sought after some advice as to care for the creature. However, upon showing a store employee what was under his coat, he was met with screams and threats to call the police. The homunculus seemed more confused than agitated by this exchange, though cautiously clung to Simon's shirt for security. Simon left in a huff—there was another pet store further down the street where, without revealing the creature, he could buy clothes intended for rodents that the homunculus might wear. A plaid vest would make him look quite distinguished, Simon thought. Simon liked vests but always forgot to look for one while shopping with Edith.

Simon and his little creature made stealthy furtive motions over the following few days. At work, Simon claimed to be gaining weight, and so kept the little thing under his shirt and cardigan (the homunculus breathed through the gaps between the buttons). The homunculus would remain surprisingly still—though, of course, sometimes needed to move. Simon learned to detect these movements before they occurred, shifting as if it were his own body, and thus performing spastic jerks in his office chair. Likewise, the usually reticent creature would sometimes make unintelligible utterances that Simon masked with coughs and dillydally babel.

Luckily, this creature seemed to be house-broken and visited the toilet whenever Simon did, resting cautiously on the rim of the bowl with surprising agility. Simon made every excuse to be at home at different times as Edith, like "two ships passing in the night." Even so, dinners and early eves Simon was obliged to spend with Edith. During this time, he put the homunculus in a shoebox poked with many holes for air, kept in a closet where it could not be heard. After Edith would fall asleep, Simon would rescue the poor thing—for a few hours at least. Upon opening the shoebox, the little man in his dapper attire would always pop up to standing, seemingly in good spirits. Perhaps it needed a good set of pajamas, Simon thought.

Then came the week's end and Simon was forced to isolate the poor creature for long hours. He visited it whenever he could break free from Edith without being suspected. He brought it to the bathroom as often as he could, and he fed it cheese, crackers, and dried fruits. A water dish lay in one corner of the shoebox and the homunculus would lick at it. However, by Sunday the water level got too low, and so the little thing had to slurp loudly.

"What's that damn noise we keep hearing?" Edith said.

"Huh? I don't hear anything—have you checked the mailbox lately?" Simon said.

"Nope."

"Aren't you expecting a package?"

"Nope."

"Do you mind looking for me? I twisted my ankle walking home yesterday and the stairs aggravate it."

"Sure!" Edith tossed the magazine she was looking at and left abruptly. Simon filled the homunculus's water dish. When Edith returned, she dropped a bundle of mail onto the kitchen table as if it were made of stone tablets. Her breath was unnecessarily audible, as if she were a Sherpa come to base camp.

"Was there anything for me?" Simon said.

"Yep," Edith said.

"What was it?" Edith ignored the question. Simon walked over, feigning a slight limp. Sifting through the mail he soon came to a letter from home. He read and then began to tremble, holding back tears. "My mother says my dog is very ill, she thinks he's dying."

"I'm sorry," Edith said. She was sitting, reading where she had left-off prior to checking the mail.

"I'm not sure why she didn't just call me, something to do with their house, I suspect. I should go and see him."

Edith did not look up, her eyes faced forward and widened sardonically. "Mmm-hmm," she said. Simon nearly began a plea for understanding but he lacked the strength. He could only think of his dog, Mumford. Simon sighed deeply but silently, concealed from Edith.

The next day, Simon journeyed by train to his hometown. The homunculus he kept tucked under his cardigan, breathing through the gaps between the buttons. His childhood home was once only a block from the station, though no longer. No one in his family was quite sure as to when it started, but one day the station seemed farther away, and this distance continued to expand. Simon knew he had to walk to where the house was when he last visited, a year ago—from there he would discover a new route. Simon went by the same landmarks he had known the previous year, past the sidewalk that ended suddenly, where the home used to be. The markers beyond he remembered: a large oak, an abandoned fence, the rusty skeleton of a van, a rope hanging from the limb of a big fir tree, swinging out into nothing.

Then Simon came to unfamiliar territory. He looked for a path that perhaps had formed in the grass and indeed noticed a thin but visible trail. There was thick prickly brush near many sections of the trail, and so Simon often had to duck under the pokey branches along his hike. He wondered why his family did not prune-back the vegetation, why they preferred to suffer needlessly. Or maybe they hardly left home, he thought. Perhaps he would take a machete to the bramble during his stay, he thought.

Not far beyond the bushes was his family home, though Simon noticed a clear difference: the house seemed much smaller and, on three sides, blue tarpaulin walls were tied down by mildewy ropes. The blue walls billowed slightly in the breeze that intermittently gusted. Simon wanted to knock on the front door but could not find where that was.

"Hello?" Simon said.

"Hello?" Came the voice of his mother, agitated and forceful.

"Hi, let me in!" Simon said.

"Who's there?" said his mother. "Who's there?!"

"It's me!"

"Who is this?—I told you no!" said his mother.

"What? ... How do I get in?" Simon said.

"NO!"

"She said no, what's wrong with you?" came a male voice—likely Franklin, her boyfriend, Simon thought.

"What the hell?" Simon said.

"I have a machete!" said the male voice.

"It's Simon, your son, who else?—you wrote to me!"

"Steven?!—go away!" said his mother.

"She told you to stop coming here, I'm getting the machete!" said the man.

"S-i-m-o-n!"

"Oh, god!" said his Mother, followed by murmurings between her and the male voice. Then the old damp ropes that held back the tarpaulin wall shook with great force. There was a violent tugging coming from the other side, mixed with unintelligible expletives. And then it all came loose. Franklin lifted up the tarpaulin, smiling.

"Hey Simon," he said.

Simon stepped inside, so distracted by the strange exchange that he forgot he was hiding his homunculus. The bushy woods surrounding their little house was dark and dank, shading out the day. A cloud had moved over head during their dialogue; the woods had dimmed and it had started to rain. The wet cold was seeping into Simon's body from the feet up, rising from the toes through the whole foot and up into the shin. Inside there was a special type of warmth that suggested sleep and reminded him of his childhood—something that he always forgot about until he was home. The lighting was low, blankets were tucked in over a neatly made settee-bed, and the house decor was overwhelmed by filagree and earth tones, though tightly filling the entire space. Several tall stacks of books provided extra shelving for odds and ends. There was a path through the clutter that Simon walked through to sit on one of the two chairs by a small table in the kitchen, where his mother had a pot of tea still hot. They hugged, though Simon made it very brief so as not to crush the tiny man he just recalled was under his cardigan.

"Would you like some tea?" she said.

Simon sat down and yawned deeply from a profound exhaustion he had exhaustingly avoided recognizing.

"Sure, thanks," Simon said.

Simon did not know what to say next. Everyone was acting as though things were normal and he lacked the energy to deviate from that behavior. He figured his mother had some dealings with a Steven that went south, but he did not possess the mental strength to listen to such a story. He kept quiet.

"Where's Mumford?" Simon said.

His mother seemed to be avoiding the subject and kept making physical excuses to not be seated, fidgeting with random doodads in the small kitchen. She did not seem to have heard Simon's question.

"Mom, could you please sit down and talk to me."

His mother sighed and shook her head in preparation for something she had clearly rehearsed. Franklin approached and stood by the table as she sat down.

"Where's my dog?"

Simon's mother again shook her head with a sigh.

"He's still incarcerated, we—"

"Wait... he's... what?"

"Simon, he—"

"You put him in a kennel or something?"

"No, listen, he was arrested, he—"

"What? No. He's a dog!"

"Deputy Larry Tart got him," Franklin said.

"Hold on, a police officer?"

"They have nothing better to do here," Franklin said.

"Just tell me what actually happened," Simon said.

"OK, look, Mumford wandered one day—"

"Why did you let him—"

"He had never done that before! Listen, he was picked up by the police and they have him in custody."

"But why?"

"He was arrested!"

"I still don't understand that, but even so, why?"

"Because he was out!"

"Why didn't they just look at his tag and bring him home?"

"They don't do that anymore," Franklin said.

"OK, well, why haven't you gone to get him?"

"We've been going to see him every day," Franklin said.

"So why haven't you brought him home?"

"They won't let you do that, Simon, it doesn't work that way anymore," said his mother.

"This is ridiculous, you just go to the shelter and prove you're the owner, or just adopt him, we have to do this now or they'll euthanize him!"

Franklin and Simon's mother both scoffed, turning their heads to the side for dramatic effect.

"That's it, where is he being kenneled? I'm going to go get him... When we moved to the city I thought he belonged here in the woods, I was wrong, apartment life is clearly better than whatever this is."

"He's not being kenneled," Franklin said.

"What the hell are you talking about?!" Simon said.

"He was arrested!" said Simon's mother.

"Are you saying he's in jail, as in... *jail...*?"

"... yes," Franklin said.

"His sentence ends the day after tomorrow, and we have to pick him up as soon as he's released, at noon, or he'll be arrested again, immediately," said Simon's mother.

"I don't understand," Simon said.

"That's how they're doing it now here, it's a crime to be a dog," Franklin said.

"You said he was sick?"

Simon's mother issued out a heavy, painful exhalation, as if there was something taut and aching within.

"Simon, he's *very* sick, we—"

"Has he seen a vet? Did he get sick there or before?"

"Julia came with us last time, she looked at him," Franklin said.

"OK, she *used* to be a vet—what's wrong with him? How and when did he get sick?"

"We think he's too old to be on that cold hard concrete, he's not getting up to his food or water much, so he has become very weak," said Simon's mother. "We tried to get them to put the cot mattress on the floor for him but they said if he can't jump up to it they won't move it for him."

"What if he can't walk out of the cell?"

"What do you mean?"

"What if he's too weak to get up on his own, can we go in and assist him, or would an officer do that?"

"I don't know," said Simon's mother.

"Of course you don't—we need to figure out these details!"

"We will, we will. Look, we're going to have to go there tomorrow and ask them lots of questions, OK?"

"We'll figure it out, Simon," Franklin said.

Simon hung his head and night took on its shape. Simon would have to sleep on the floor, the next day his mother was to show him how to get to the northern section of the house. The house had not diminished in size, like he thought, but was separating into sections, ever expanding outward from the central portion where they were. Simon learned that, fortunately, horse-drawn carriages now drove by at regular intervals during the day, on a dirt road he had not noticed prior. He could hitch a ride to other parts of the house—the northern section had a spare bedroom with some of his old stuff.

Simon stepped outside, beyond the tarpaulin contraption, to get some air. He remembered, suddenly, about the homunculus. Frantically he undid his cardigan and picked up the poor creature. It had a stale hopeless look on its face, and it had soiled itself. Simon set it down on the ground to get a better look by the light of the kitchen window.

"I'm so sorry," Simon said.

At that moment, the homunculus perked up, its eyes bulged, and it let out a strange wail, as if a cat had swallowed a loquacious toad. Simon gasped and then the creature ran off, disappearing into the dark woods. Simon hunched his shoulders and, dejected, returned indoors.

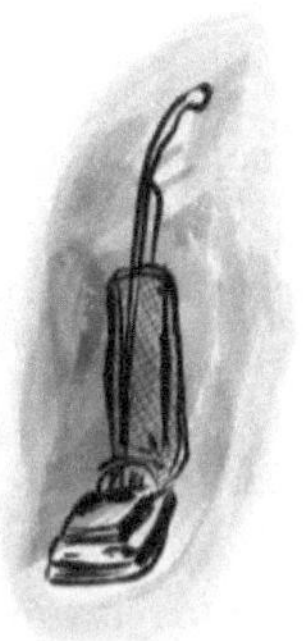

THE VACUUM

The crows were restless that day. They exhibited a behavior known officially as "cacophonous aggregation," usually occurring in the presence of a dead conspecific; when one or more crows gather around a fallen comrade and skold (a guttural squawk repeated in short concessions). These calls differ contextually from a simple alarm call to signal danger—the phenomenon is truly a crow funeral (of sorts), though the exact function of the behavior, and whether crows actually possess a

complex understanding of death, is unknown. (How appropriate that a "murder of crows" can also be a funeral).

The crows were restless that day. They skolded and they skolded. They had circled the suburban house all morning; an incredible fluttering of wings, a great black mass, a ravenous, murderous funeral of crows. One of their species had hit a window in its flight and fallen dead in the backyard: a thick brown entanglement of weeds along a faded wood fence, a brief lawn with patches of dirt, and a rusty unloved trampoline. The garden, once kept in a state of resplendent beauty by its previous owners, was then in dilapidated disarray. The Bungs had no time for gardening.

The rapacious vacuum cleaner sucked the remains of dinner off the living room rug like a screaming wild beast. The vacuum was wielded by Rupert Bung. Food scraps were strewn around the coffee table. His wife Margaret and their two children, Elsa and John, did not like to eat in the dining room. Rupert was told that it was his odious desire for conversation which drove them to the couch, sheltered by the television.

The vacuum was an expensive item, newly purchased at a department store. It was state-of-the-art and somewhat outside the Bung budget, what Margaret later described as a "splurge." Margaret had been complaining about their inadequate machine (an ancient one-speed clunker-sucker) for some time. Rupert maintained that he was the only person in the whole house who did any vacuuming whatsoever, and it suited him just fine. But then finally, that day at the store, Rupert capitulated to Margaret's incessant nagging. His one consolation was to have the esteemed privilege of picking out the new vacuum for himself, though limited to the high-end aisle Margaret had steered him to. An indigo blue contraption immediately caught Rupert's eye—the "Cyclone Dragon," as it was called.

His son John stared at the vacuum intently. The vacuum stood there on display in a perfect stillness John found disturbing. He envisioned an actual dragon emerging out of the vacuum with terrifying reality. The sleek curves, the sturdy switches, the pumps and levers, and all the bells and whistles began to morph into dragon scales, teeth, and claws. When Rupert moved the display in inspection, the sudden jerking motion startled the boy, as if flames from the dragon's breath would have engulfed them all.

It was early that following evening when Rupert began his test run of the "Cyclone Dragon." Rupert marveled at the majesty of the modern dynamo: popcorn disappeared instantly within a meter of Rupert's approach; wrappers, cauliflower the children had flicked from their dinner plates, bits of corn dogs, doll heads, long hairs woven into rug fibers, embedded dirt—all was consumed by the vacuum with extreme speed and efficiency. Rupert thought that the vacuum was the epitome of *clean* itself; an angelic machine that purified its environs with a halo of suction.

Abruptly the vacuum stopped, interrupting Rupert's elated reverie. He let out a sigh of annoyance at a moderate decibel.

"What?! What's your problem?!" yelled Margaret, in reaction to Rupert's modest display of irritation. Rupert simply ignored Margaret's outburst and leaned in to investigate the cause of the malfunction (Margaret scoffed loudly and rolled her eyes whilst orientating her chin to the ceiling).

Rupert discovered a large black feather stuck to the mouth of the great sucker, "something the dog must have brought in" Rupert thought. Rupert was somewhat disappointed that a mere feather had obstructed the suction-flow of the machine, especially after much heftier objects had been whisked away with incredible ease. Rupert soon noticed, however, that the suction strength was set to a default level of one. Relieved, and with regained confidence, Rupert gleefully advanced the strength level to two. But despite this new development, the black feather persisted to block all suction. Rupert then attempted a higher strength level of three, then higher, higher still, and so on without success. Eventually, Rupert was faced with adjusting the strength level to 10, the very last. With nervous perspiration, and trembling slightly, he set the lever to the bottom notch of 10. Heat from the machine radiated like a furnace. Gears spun wildly and pumps clanged like gongs, though still the feather was unmoved.

Rupert bent to one knee, baffled, though nevertheless resolved in doing it "the old-fashioned way," as he told himself— i.e. just simply pulling the feather out. This change in operations caused his teenaged daughter Elsa to become momentarily distracted from the television.

"Dad, what are doing?"

Rupert turned to her and smiled. Elsa raised her eyebrows in what was both an incredulous and sarcastic expression, returning her focus once more to the television. Rupert too reverted to his previous attentions and pinched the feather between his index finger and thumb. A profusion of sweat fell from his forehead to the floor and his heart pounded. He braced himself for a mighty tug: quadriceps tensed, shoulders hunched, biting his lower lip in concentration. Yet, to Rupert's surprise and amazement, the feather broke free from the jaws of the vacuum with little more effort than picking up a piece of paper. However, the extra force he had applied to the great yank tossed him onto his back with a thud, feather in hand.

"Oh my god," Margaret exclaimed in obvious vexation.

"I've had just about all that I can take," muttered Rupert under his breath.

"Excuse me?" inquired Margaret after Rupert's whisper.

Rupert's skin became flush, heat rose to his scalp and his eyes bulged in their sockets. As these internal responses to emotional stimuli occurred, the vacuum seemed to mimic Rupert's physiology as it revved, sputtered, cranked, and screeched, still set to level 10. An undone shoelace of Rupert's inched toward the suction as he lay on the floor. Margaret stared at Rupert unfazed, her upper lip curled, and eyes widened, ready for anything. Margaret was always confident in her incendiary talent for rebuttal, most often imbued with sharp and unshakeable indignation.

Rupert stuttered over an opening statement in the spotlight of Margaret's glare. Typically, his flustering would have been the end of it, but this time was different, this time he managed to pause, draw in a breath, and collect himself. He decided then, at that very moment, he was ready to speak, to truly speak. Perhaps for the first time in his life, he was genuinely committed, nothing was to be held back.

"I SAID!!!—"

Rupert's catharsis was immediately cut short. The Cyclone Dragon gave out a deafening bellow and suddenly he vanished, sucked into the mechanical void. Though his body was inhaled in a flash, it appeared to his son John to have the same plasticity as that of a used lunch sack; a wrinkled and soggy piece of paper rubbish that collapsed its compostable fibers in an almost melancholic yield to the great suck. Once Rupert was consumed, the Cyclone Dragon shook spastically, let out a plume of soot, and then stopped all together. The outlet it was connected to had sparked and shorted, cutting power both to the vacuum and the television. Floating to the ground where Rupert had lain but an instant earlier was the feather, drifting through the ephemeral moment in a cloud of dust. Margaret and the children passed a full minute completely frozen in bewilderment over what they had just witnessed.

John was the first to break the silence: "Dad?" he said in a gravelly voice, holding back frightened tears.

Elsa let out a chilling shriek that provoked John to sob hysterically.

Margaret, stunned and agasp, did not make a sound, shocked beyond herself. She knew what she had seen, she knew that the children were reacting to something dreadful like what she had seen, but she just could not bring herself to believe it. She could not break her impervious sense of logic. Residing thus in a state of perfect cognitive dissonance, Margaret was absolutely immobilized.

"Mom! Do something!" Elsa shouted.

"Huh?" Margaret said as if roused from an accidental nap.

"Do something!"

"Margaret?" came a faint moan unheard over the panic.

"Shut up!" Elsa yelled at her crying little brother. "Just shut up!"

"Elsa!" said Margaret.

"He always makes everything worse, and so do you!"

"You can't talk to me like that!"

"I hate you!"

"Margaret?" again the phantom like murmur went unnoticed.

"You're mean!" said John mid-sob.

"I hate both of you!"

"Elsa that's enough, be kind to your mother," said a stern voice. The room silenced. "Margaret? Where am I?"

At once, everyone rushed to the vacuum.

"Rupert! We're here, the children and I are right here. Are you, erm, I don't know what to say, I—"

"Are you OK?" said Elsa.

"I can't see or move, did I fall?" Rupert said, his voice shaking at the thought of being both blind and paralyzed.

"No Rupert, well, you did fall back from fiddling with the thing, or whatever, but then... Oh I don't know, I- I just don't know—"

"The vacuum sucked you up!" said Elsa.

"What? Come on, that's impossible," said Rupert.

"It's true! We all saw it happen!" said Elsa.

"Dad? Does this mean you're not going to my game?" said John.

"Well, I don't know bud, I guess it all depends on my current situation here."

"I knew you wouldn't go!" John began crying, in a whiney sort of way, and buried his head in his mother's shoulder.

"Rupert, you know how much this means to him, and you missed the last game, because you were off doing who knows what," said Margaret.

"I told you, I had an important meeting that came up last minute."

A thought then occurred to Margaret: "Rupert, is this some kind of joke? Or magic trick? Because if it is—"

"No! Honestly, I have no idea what's going on."

"How can you fit in there?" said Elsa.

"I'm not sure, I can't move but I can feel that my body is there, somehow."

"How can you breathe?" said Elsa.

"I really don't know sweetheart, the air is stuffy, tastes like chalk" (Rupert took in a sample breath and coughed) "but I can breathe, just—"

"You're a liar!" said John.

"What's that buddy?"

"You said you'd go to my game, you lied, you always lie!"

"Listen champ, your game's not until the weekend, right? So, I'll just call in sick the rest of the week and who knows, maybe I can sleep this off."

"Whatever," said John.

"Margaret, can you explain to him—"

"I'm not bailing you out of this one, Rupert. He has a point, you know—this is a pattern of behavior you need to fix."

"You need to fix a pattern, Dad!" said John.

Rupert mumbled a little tisk-tisk.

"What was that, Rupert? Did you have something to say to your son, who loves you and looks up to you and expects his hero to cheer him on and support him at his important game?"

"Chief, let's just see how this goes, I want nothing more than to attend your game, and watch you score big-time, and I'm going to do everything in my power to make sure that happens, OK buddy?"

"I guess," said John.

"I think we all just need to go to bed," said Rupert.

"Ugh, I thought you were going to fix the T.V.," said Elsa.

"Just use the one in your room sweetie," said Rupert.

"Uh, it's broken, remember? That's what I'm talking about."

"Watch the one in your brother's room," said Rupert.

"No, she's not allowed in my room!"

"Just forget it, as usual," said Elsa. "I have my phone, it's all I have."

"Why does she get a phone and I don't?" said John. "It's so unfair."

Margaret clapped her hands, bringing attention to her well-anticipated decree: "Alright kids, you heard your father, it's time for bed—right now!"

And so, the Bung children marched sulkily upstairs to their respective rooms. Rupert and Margaret's bedroom was on the ground floor, which proved convenient as Margaret had to push Rupert's heavy body in the Cyclone Dragon. Once in their room, Margaret (a little out of breath) began her routine. Her nightly ritual was, for the Bungs, a tacitly affectionate time, wherein Margaret would undress and put on her night gown, and Rupert would sit on the bed and admire her. Margaret would then sit in front of her vanity, slowly remove her makeup, and search for elusive bobby-pins whilst combing her long, luscious locks. As she did this, Rupert too would change into his pajamas, and they would talk. Their talk was most often soft and banal—regardless of what spats or quarrels they might have had previously in the day. On this night, however, there was a degree of tension that lingered in the air. Rupert could only imagine Margaret's tender movements that he so looked forward to, one of the last intimate aspects of their marriage.

"Oh Rupert, what are we going to do with you?"

"I don't know how this happened. I thought I read the manual well enough, it didn't mention anything like this."

"Why do I feel as though I'm always bailing you out?"

"I didn't mean for any of this, Margaret."

"We're just going to have to go see Dr. Mortimer in the morning. I'm not sure what else to do when you have this kind of accident. I'll have to call in sick from work, not as though that's really an option for me but I'll have to. You can't drive or take care of the kids like this."

"'Accident'? So, you don't blame me?"

"Rupert, I don't blame you, I'm worried about you. I just wish you didn't keep making these little mistakes that have huge consequences. Like when you backed into the hardware store and broke their window. I had to sell some stuff of mine just to pay for that, or else we wouldn't have been able to afford our vacation."

"I thought you just exchanged my ticket?"

"Yes Rupert, and I had to sell my grandfather's old cameras to Janice's husband, who I guess has some sort of collection, you don't remember? Otherwise we wouldn't have been able to afford to be there. It certainly wasn't easy traveling with two kids by myself, I couldn't really enjoy my vacation. It was their vacation."

"I missed you guys."

"Yeah right, you probably had a blast here by yourself for ten days."

"That's not true... I'm sorry it was stressful; we should have just gone all together the following year."

"I couldn't disappoint our children Rupert, which seems easy for you."

"Are you talking about the game?"

"What else?"

"Like I said—"

"Oh, I take that back, there are several 'elses.' You know what, let's just forget it, I'm too tired for this."

Margaret turned out the lights. Rupert did not notice the lights go out, for him it was already dark. He instead heard the familiar click of the switch and in his mind he turned out the lights.

"Good night," said Rupert.

Margaret sighed and mumbled something like "good night."

Rupert did not sleep, though he experienced a peculiar form of rest, as if dozing in the delirium of a fever, without body, floating through an endless black. Though sometimes a dreamlike image would appear, shimmering from a pellucid well within the limitless dark expanse.

The sun soon rose. Dappled light fluttered in through their open bedroom window. By then, dust inside the dragon had settled just enough for Rupert to make out the smell of morning dew. With its fragrance came the memory of dawn's luminous glow upon his face, still and tranquil. Margaret, on the other hand, awoke with a frantic gasp for air, seconds before her alarm. Hastily she prepared breakfast, called the kids' schools to be excused for the day, informed both their jobs of a family emergency, and rang Dr. Mortimer's clinic, begging for a same-day appointment.

Margaret carted Rupert into the kitchen near the breakfast table, without a word. The children ate their breakfast mostly in silence, not talking beyond a murmur. Elsa glumly stared at her phone, into that intoxicatingly uninteresting little screen, and John watched cartoons on Margaret's laptop computer. Rupert could smell the pancakes they smacked down, could taste the aroma of maple syrup, could hear the coffeemaker percolating through the grounds, and the eggs sizzling in butter. Rupert then became profoundly aware of his hunger, for not only was his stomach (wherever it was) severely empty but he did not know when next he would eat, if ever again. In that moment, the possibility of starvation was real and tangible. A true sense of panic ensued, though he did not voice it. Rupert had not yet attempted to speak to anyone that morning and he wondered if his voice had indeed disappeared, if perhaps the Dragon had swallowed that up as well.

Immediately following breakfast, Margaret received a call from the clinic informing her that Dr. Mortimer would see them that morning. Quickly she ushered the family to the garage and hoisted Rupert into their SUV (with reluctant help from the children), taking care to strap his seat belt around the Dragon's awkward shape.

Once checked into the clinic, Margaret spent a painful half hour waiting to be seen, enduring awkward glances and scowls from the other patients. Elsa, though usually prone to embarrassment, remained somewhat oblivious whilst fidgeting with the unremarkable world offered up by her phone. John also kept himself occupied, but with a video game. Margaret was much too tense for any kind of distraction, she managed only to stare beyond the other patients' silent inquisition, transfixed upon the door from which the nurse would come. Rupert, feeling hungrier still, endeavored to conserve his energy and keep his anxiety at bay. He guessed that they had arrived at the clinic, and so he told himself to simply wait and see what the doctor would say.

When the Bung name was finally called, the nurse showed the family to their room and proceeded to ask the usual questions, to which Rupert groaned his answers from inside the Dragon. Out of some struggle to maintain an air of composure, the nurse then ventured to take Rupert's vitals. Fumbling and uncoordinated, however, the nurse soon gave surrender to the words: "OK, the doctor will see you shortly," and darted out the door. Rupert was surprised that he still possessed the ability to speak, though his volume was weakened, and this alone produced a hint of optimism that swept over him.

After a brief knock, Dr. Mortimer stepped into the room with frenetic and purposeful energy. His presence was evidenced to Rupert by the strong odor of sanitizer, swishing about as he vigorously rubbed his hands together. He greeted the family in a polite but performative tone, offering a damp sterile handshake to Margaret and each of the two kids, but stopped at Rupert.

"Well looks like we'll have to take a raincheck on that handshake Roop."

"It's a date," said Rupert.

"Ah, you can still talk, that's very reassuring," said Dr. Mortimer. He sat down and glanced over Rupert's chart. "Looks like the nurse skipped over your vitals there Roop, but I guess we'll have to give him a pass on that one today," he said with a chuckle.

"Can you please tell us what's going on?" said Margaret.

"We'll get to that, but first I want to do my best at determining his vitals—Did you hear that Roop? We're going to give it the old college try and get some vitals."

Dr. Mortimer then listened with his stethoscope all over the vacuum, trying his best to discover "the sweet spot," as he called it.

"Well, Roop," he said, "your vitals, as far as I can ascertain—and of course, I am limited here—are perfectly normal. I can't hear anything to raise concern over your heart or your lungs. Now, I would like to fit you in for an Xray before you leave the clinic and get a closer look at things, but I assume what we'll find is something like the other cases, where the body is essentially held in a vacuum of pressure—hey, no pun intended there buddy—and somehow this condenses everything, yet your body remains functional."

"Other cases?" said Margaret. John, who had just fallen asleep on Margaret's shoulder, let out a soft snort.

"Yes, so what we have here guys—"

"Huh?" Elsa furrowed her brow and peeked over her phone.

"Hey there, glad you could join us. Yeah, so what's happened here is very simple: Rupert, your body is contained under high pressure by a popular household appliance known as the Cyclone Serpent—no, excuse me, Dragon. Now, we don't understand fully how it happens or how the victim is able to remain alive, and this is still a very recent phenomenon, yet we do know of a few ways that allow the patient to cope with the circumstances."

"So, this has happened before?" said Margaret.

"Oh yes, since last spring, when the product was made commercially available in the U.S., there have been 219 recorded incidents. There are more worldwide, though I'm not sure how many. All European countries have already banned sale of the product, as well as China, Japan, Canda, Israel, Australia, New Zealand, Mexico, almost all of South America, India, Pakistan, and Namibia, if I remember correctly. The U.S. will soon follow."

"Did they survive?" said Rupert.

"What was that Roop?"

"The other cases, did they survive?"

"Ah, yes—well, it's perhaps too soon to tell, but 217 out of the 219 incidents are currently surviving, yes."

"Why can't you just remove him from the Serpent Whirlpool thing?" said Margaret.

"Oh, well, those two who didn't make it... need I say more? We don't truly understand it, and it's still very early, but extracting the patient from the Serpent has been known to be fatal. That's not to say we won't find some way of getting you outta there in the future, Roop. But at this point, it's hard to say when that will be... It may take a while."

"How can I eat?"

"OK Roop, let's get you informed as to what you need to know going forward. And, Margaret, this will include the help of family. That is crucial. If family is unable to help then, well Roop, you'll need to be taken into convalescence. Which can be expensive. So, this information is for you guys as much as it is for Rupert."

"Of course, we're here to help," said Margaret, her eyes bulging somewhat. John stirred in his dozing and moved his head to his mother's lap. Elsa thumbed her phone's screen and slouched in her chair.

"Great, so how do you eat? Well, Roop, we've discovered that you can eat soft foods, at about the same consistency as apple sauce. You do this by simply placing the food at the mouth of the Serpent (which is where your family comes in)," Dr. Mortimer looked to Margaret and murmured: "you have to put the food on the floor—lay down some tinfoil so it's sanitary."

"Then what?" said Rupert.

"Then pucker up your lips, Roop, and slurp as hard as you can. This may take some practice as you're in the dark there... Oh, and I suggest smoothies and savory soups to make sure you get enough nutrition—but take care not to scald yourself, you have to let the soup cool down first."

"What about going to the bathroom?" said Rupert.

"Ew Dad, gross," said Elsa.

"An important question to be sure. Well, Roop, we're not sure how it works but you just go, and amazingly the waste is transported to the lint chamber on the outside, just there," Dr. Mortimer pointed to the clear cylinder attached to the side of the

Dragon. "You'll see it fill up, and, you just have to detach it and dump it in the toilet."

"Oh my god," said Margaret.

"Yep, it's not pretty but it's convenient, and it keeps him alive," said Dr. Mortimer. "Not sure how the waste gets beyond your clothes, but it's thought that your clothing actually gets torn from your body in the split second prior to being consumed by the Serpent."

"What about my breathing, am I going to run out of air?"

"Nope, no no no, what we've found—"

"Are we going to have to push Dad around?" said Elsa.

"Actually, no. You'll have to refer to your manual but there's a feature that electronically drives the Serpent. And Roop, you might be able to control it. Not all cases, but most, have been able to drive the Serpent themselves."

"How?" said Rupert.

"We honestly don't know, but they're able to do it. Just make sure your battery is charged and the function is switched on. But you'll need a guide, you don't want to drive blind across a busy street."

"This is a lot to take in," said Rupert.

"You're alive Roop, that's what you need to remind yourself. This is a very new phenomenon, so you just have to take things day by day, and we're going to be here with you every step of the way... For now, I'm giving you, Margaret, a packet that reiterates what I've gone over with you guys today, and if you ever have any questions just give us a call here at the clinic. If, Roop, you start to experience any symptoms that concern you I want you to come into the clinic ASAP, OK? And as it is, I would like to follow up with an appointment one week from now."

"What are people doing about the company that sold the vacuums, shouldn't they cover our costs at the very least?" said Margaret.

"Well, I actually have another patient in your shoes, or should I say vacuum," Dr. Mortimer let out a brief chuckle, "and while I can't break any confidentiality, I know that they have been very very successful, and I mean *very* successful, with the advice I'm about to give you..." Dr. Mortimer paused for dramatic effect.

"What's that?" said Margaret.

"Get a lawyer, a good one."

That night, Rupert drifted once more between sleep and waking, floating in the same feverish limbo he had experienced the evening prior, as hunger prevented any hope for deep rest. Rupert had done his best to slurp up the gruel Margaret had made for him at dinner, but he was nevertheless famished (she would have prepared a more significant meal, but going to the doctor and dealing with the kids was all that she could "handle" for that day). His stomach rumbled like a freight train, the sounds of which reverberated throughout his dark chamber.

Suddenly, Margaret awoke, springing to a seated position as if catapulted out of sleep. "Rupert? Darling, are you awake?" She switched on the bedside lamp.

"Sorry, did my belly wake you? It's been gurgling so incredibly loud, or at least it's loud in here."

"I don't think so. I didn't hear anything—but I had the most vivid dream, like a vision."

"What about?"

"The Serpent—"

"Dragon."

"What?"

"Dragon, everybody keeps calling it 'Serpent' but it's Dragon."

"Oh, yeah, the Dragon Hurricane, or whatever, I had a dream about it."

"What happened?" Rupert's voice trembled slightly, nervous about what Margaret might say.

"You had turned into a meatball, a flying meatball that hovered above us. I knew it was you, it had your face, somehow. We were all in the living room, where it happened. And the Hurricane was there. I think it spat you out like that, but it was still connected to you, in some way..."

"Oh god."

"Wait, I'm not done... Then the dog came into the room. He was jumping up at you, trying to eat you! But you, you flew out the door. Then Rusty chased after you. We all followed, we ran outside. It was a sort of eerie in-between day and night, I'm not sure how to describe it..."

"Like twilight?"

"Kind of, but different, and the streets had all turned into meadows and woods. We ran and ran until finally you and Rusty came to a cliff. The dog stopped but you fell, even though before you could fly. I shouted out and then, I don't know how, I was at the bottom of the cliff. It was dark down there, but I had a flashlight and I looked for you. Then I found... oh Rupert—"

"What is it?" Rupert's teeth chattered as he spoke.

"There was this beautiful glimmer of light, a pool of light, almost unnatural but so so beautiful. I knew what it was, it was where you had hit the bottom, it was what you had become. I got closer to it and, whew, the light shone from a magnificent mound of gold!"

"Gold?"

"Yes Rupert, gold! Oh Rupert, I have never felt more optimistic than I do now. We're going to fix this honey, and I know this has been awful for you, oh I feel so sorry for you darling, but what I realize now is that this is truly a blessing in disguise—we're going to be so rich!"

"You really think so?"

"You heard what the doctor said, about his other patient. We need to get ourselves a lawyer, Rupert, a good one... Oh Rupert, I can hardly wait until tomorrow!"

As excited as Margaret was, she found it easy to go back to sleep. Rupert, on the other hand, was unable to even doze. He recalled his usual experience with insomnia, how ceaselessly through the night he would toss and turn from one aggravatingly uncomfortable position to another—oh how he wished he could still do that! The supreme restraint of the Dragon became more real and tangible than it ever had before, like an unbearable straight jacket. Rupert promptly came to the verge of panic, his anxiety ready to erupt in anyway it could, to explode out of the Dragon in his intense desire to move, even if it meant dying in the process.

Rupert was but a moment from letting out an extraordinary scream when Margaret began to snore softly. It was a gentle sort of snore, a soothing snore that for Rupert seemed to originate from a peaceful, almost primordial place, like water rippling on a calm shore. The snore called to his mind the image of boats, bobbing and drifting through a luminescent radiance of midday light on water. Rupert held to this image until morning; he sailed on a calm idyllic bay and breathed the sea air. He brought Margaret and the two children with him there. They were laughing there, smiling in the bright sunlight and kissed by a kind breeze. The optimism Margaret had felt earlier filtered through like the light itself. Perhaps she was right, Rupert thought, perhaps sailing was a vision of their future, a future of leisure and the tranquil enjoyment of each other's company, and he would give it all to them. He was not sure, but in that moment he suspected tears, tears of happiness at the thought of it.

Breakfast was different than the day before. Margaret, though again focused and purposeful with her movements, had nevertheless relaxed. She took extra time to prepare Rupert's gruel. She announced each ingredient she tossed into the blender, hoping that she might provide Rupert with as normal a meal in taste as possible: waffle with butter and syrup, corn flakes, and an omelet. For drink: orange juice and cold brew coffee.

"Oh my god Dad! Gross!" said Elsa.

"I'm sorry sweetie, it must be the coffee," said Rupert. Margaret gave no protestation and quickly took the lint chamber to the bathroom and dumped the waste.

"OK Princess, let me ask you a question," said Rupert. Elsa gave no response.

"Did you hear that sweetie?" said Rupert.

"Answer your father!" said Margaret.

"Uh, what's that Dad? Jeez," said Elsa.

"If you could have anything for that big birthday coming up, what would you want?"

"Are you serious?"

"That's right, if you could have anything what would it be?"

"I guess I'd want a car"

"Just any car?"

"I don't know, a Porsche."

"OK, good to know."

"Is this for real?"

"You'll just have to wait and see," said Rupert.

Elsa had an expression on her face Margaret had not seen in years: her eyes glinted in the morning light like shimmering blue sapphires, and under those eyes she wore a childishly innocent smile, one that was still in love with the world. Margaret placed a hand on the Dragon and also began to smile—the gentle smile of one who was still in love with their marriage. She knew then that Rupert shared her hopes.

Rupert's optimistic euphoria carried him through the day and thus allowed him to focus on learning about his "new life," as he told himself. Margaret had already charged the battery to the Dragon since the Doctor's visit, and so his aim was to discover the driving feature that would allow him to move freely. He inched what could have been a finger towards a number of bumps and lumps inside the Dragon, testing an applied pressure to each protrusion. After many trials, he finally felt the Dragon jolt abruptly. Their dog yelped in alarm and Rupert felt the impact of something hard against the Dragon, stopping his motion. He cried out with exalted joy at his achievement, unintelligible but nevertheless something like a "eureka."

"Hey Rusty, do you want to go for a walk? Just a matter of time now buddy." The dog responded with a confused tilt of his ruddy head. Rupert toiled vigorously within the Dragon to find reverse, shaking the Dragon slightly with his movements. Rusty began to growl, which prompted Rupert to laugh. He did not quite know why he laughed, but his laughter filled him with a sense of exultant glee, as if he had triumphed at last.

Margaret returned from work late that afternoon, having picked up the Bung children from their extracurricular practices. They found Rupert wedged between the couch and end table, laughing hysterically, whilst Rusty barked at the Dragon in a frantic and desperate manner. There was some sharp chastising that came immediately from Margaret, which quickly transformed into an expression of concern once she remembered the change in attitude she had recently adopted. Exhausted, though again renewed by this fresh outlook, she suggested going out to dinner. Normally such an expenditure for the Bungs would be reserved solely for a special occasion. Yet, Margaret knew that this was, indeed, a time to celebrate; a time to relish tacitly in their bright future before informing the children of their prospects. Moreover, she was much too tired to cook for everyone—a point she often made when whipping up dinner despite her evening fatigue (used as a plea for sympathy from the Bungs, though much to her chagrin).

The Bung family dined at their favorite restaurant, Meat o' Balls. It was an Italian food chain with good service, moderate prices, and predictable food. The interior of the place was bedecked by a stained glass and chandelier theme, reminiscent of an old Art Deco train station. The prevalence of colored glass glistened like a carousal of luminescence. The din of clinking dishes and cutlery, typical for a large and popular restaurant of its kind, was cushioned by the sparkling glow of it all, transmogrified into what was pleasing to the Bung ear—possessing all the charm and enchantment of wind chimes in a soft breeze. Plastic vines and roses adorned the tables and many nooks and crannies throughout the restaurant's wide space, supplying the Bungs with a sort of still comfort; a clean and immaculate beauty that neither faded nor needed any care.

The restaurant staff were very accommodating to Rupert, as if they were familiar with his situation, and so took no issue in blending his minestrone soup at room temperature. The waiter laid down tinfoil for Rupert with the same balletic maneuver as changing a table cloth. For the first time since his accident, Rupert felt the confidence of being normal. Inspired, he ventured to reassume his fatherly presence at the table, perhaps with even an air of authority, despite his being on the floor below.

"More water there guy?" asked their server.

"Yeah," said John, pointing to his empty glass.

"*Yes please*, son, say *yes please*," said Rupert.

"Yeah please," said John.

As the server poured the water, Elsa shouted: "Look mom! Some people are actually sitting there tonight—under the gazebo!"

"What?!" said Margaret.

At the center of the restaurant, elevated two meters above the floor, was a large gazebo with a roof of plastic ivy woven into its lattice work. From its pinnacle hung an ornate candelabra, suspended above a table and floor composed entirely of stained glass—an iridescent mosaic that seemed to dance with the lights overhead, spinning like a dervish. The gazebo had been something of a Bung family mystery. It baffled the Bungs as to why they never saw anyone at the gazebo, or why the host never offered to seat them there. The enigma would have no doubt been easily solved had Margaret or Rupert simply asked a Meat o' Balls employee about the gazebo, but they felt much too embarrassed to do so. They hypothesized that it was expensive and by reservation only, and that perhaps only the rich and famous ever dined there. That on this night (of all possible nights) there were people seated under the gazebo, sent a shock down Margaret's spine, though she had not yet turned to look and verify Elsa's claim. She sensed it as fate, which roused a cryptic kind of apprehension in her, the likes of which she had only ever felt before in dreams. Internally, she chided herself for her irrational and vague fear, then spun around to confront the gazebo.

To Margaret's amazement, she saw two children (roughly the same age as her own) and an elderly couple (presumably the grandparents), all sitting alongside a *vacuum* (that looked very much like what had swallowed Rupert). Margaret stared at them intently. The grandfather noticed her and their eyes met. Margaret remained still, transfixed, as though utterly compelled to look at them. The grandfather nudged his wife and then they both looked at Margaret. Smiling knowingly, they nodded and raised their wine glasses to her. Margaret responded with a cheers from her own glass of soda and then her focus returned to her table. A wave of positivity blanketed her, warming her hands that before she had thought were cold.

"Well? Who is up there? A movie star?" said Rupert, chuckling a bit.

"No Rupert, they're just ordinary people, people like us... They're people like us who just sat under the gazebo!" said Margaret.

That night, Margaret glided through their bedtime routine with an air of smug sophistication. Her attitude emerged from the pretense of having just ascended into a higher stratum of society, a class that Margaret would later describe as not only natural but destined for them. It was as if they had already themselves dined under the gazebo at Meat o' Balls.

Enchanting though it was, her fantastical mood was rudely interrupted once Rupert's lint chamber filled suddenly with an exuberant burst of energy. "I'm sorry, I must be nervous about this whole lawyer business," said Rupert.

Margaret put up an invisible fence which protected her from ugly things. She did not wish to break the magic spell that hung about her like an incandescent aura. She took the lint chamber and disposed of the waste with perfect detachment. From the bathroom

Margaret spoke to Rupert with a far removed yet whimsical tone, a voice imbued with noble matter-of-factness. She informed Rupert that she had talked to a coworker that day who knew of an excellent lawyer by the name of Grundle, one who had a reputation for "defending the consumer."

"So don't be nervous. Remember, this company of the... the Serpent-thing, has violated your rights, Rupert, not only as a consumer but a citizen, and now it is absolutely within your right to demand compensation, and I'm talking monetary compensation, and lots of it," said Margaret. "You're a victim Rupert, a victim, and now it's time for them to be held responsible and cover your losses. And just think about it, no matter how much money they compensate it doesn't even begin to make up for being trapped (indefinitely) in a vacuum, now does it?"

"No, I suppose not."

"That's why we need to make them *pay*, and I think Grundle might be our answer."

The next morning, after breakfast, Rupert enlisted the help of his son to walk their dog around the neighborhood. For a leash, Rupert had John tie the electrical cord from the vacuum to Rusty's collar. Rupert was the only person of the family who ever walked Rusty, and so it had been a few days since Rusty had roamed beyond the confines of their backyard. Pent up and unfamiliar with John as a walking companion, Rusty bolted down the sidewalk the moment John opened the front door. He ran like a rocket down the street, all the while tied to the Dragon's cord which seemed to unravel endlessly. At long last, more than a block away, the cord became in an instant taut and snapped Rusty to a halt. The Dragon remained nearly inert, somehow weighted like an anchor in response to the cord's canid sojourn. Rupert, becoming increasingly aware of the device's mechanics, then realized he knew how to retract the cord, which fiercely pulled Rusty back with rapid force. With the voice of authority Rupert shouted "heel!" and Rusty at once obeyed, appearing to have finally made the connection between Rupert and the Dragon. Calmly, they walked on, with John as the "navigator."

Rupert enjoyed walking the dog. He liked to talk to Rusty on their jaunts, sometimes about important matters but mostly he would palaver on whatever came to his mind. To his family he would say jokingly that Rusty was the only one who listened to him. Indeed, Rupert's boring thoughts were never tolerated in the house. He could not openly share his opinions about what he had read in the newspaper (whenever he was given a chance to read the newspaper), his lists of the best or worst of something, nor any so-called "random" observation of the world. He used to try, but his family would typically roll their eyes in annoyance and ignore Rupert, usually walking out of the room, even mid-sentence. Eventually Rupert learned not to bother them with his humorous ideas or idle chit chat. Because of this, the dog became the outlet for his thoughts, and he reckoned Rusty might even appreciate the sound of his voice.

When the children were much younger, they in fact did show a great deal of interest in Rusty. They would dress him in various costumes and act out elaborate make-believe scenarios in the backyard. Margaret too seemed to have loved Rusty, showing John as a toddler how to throw a ball and play fetch with the dog. Over time, these affections diminished, and Rupert was unsure as to why. He felt it strange and unnatural for a child to neglect a dog, and thought it as a sign of something wrong, though precisely what was wrong he did not know. Rupert ultimately blamed himself for his children's apathy toward their dog (really, all animals), though exactly how he was at fault he did not know. Yet as he walked Rusty with John, just a few days after being swallowed by a vacuum, Rupert began to realize that parallel to his family's affections diminishing toward the dog, so too over the years had Rupert's affections depleted toward his own family. Though for a long time Rupert had convinced himself otherwise, on this walk he could not help but admit internally that his affections had been replaced with automatic words and gestures—a force of habit lacking genuine content.

Rupert wheeled onward, detecting only the forward force of the Dragon and the propulsion of the dog's tug upon the vacuum cord. To his senses, their motion was through a dark void, but at each turn a perfect image came to his mind of where they were, for he had walked it a thousand times before. Rupert pictured every tree, hedge, and fence as Rusty moved through his habitual constitution.

He imagined theirs was a brisk march through the neighborhood on a chilly yellow-leaved day. He wondered if the leaves had yet fallen. He made his usual armchair predictions of the impending winter, guessing there would be more snow than the previous year.

Then a memory came to him, a memory Rupert had not thought of in decades. He recalled an incident from when he was at boarding school. It was winter and the first snow had just covered the ground in early evening. There was only a couple of hours before curfew, but Rupert and his roommate Sandy wanted to explore the alluringly white woods behind their dormitory. Rupert had recently purchased a book on animal tracking from the bookstore in town and it was Sandy's idea that the fresh snow might provide an excellent opportunity for identifying tracks in the forest. There was an unofficial path that the students, though not allowed to walk there, had made over the years. Both Rupert and Sandy had tromped around in the woods before but always with a lingering tension that comes with the possibility of getting caught. This year they were both seniors and so did not care. Their only focus was the task of exploration.

Not far into the woods, Rupert and Sandy spotted paw prints of some kind. They were large like a big breed of dog but square shaped and lacking the nail marks around the pads. Looking at the book with a large cheap plastic flashlight, Rupert and Sandy agreed (with much excitement) that only a mountain lion could make such a track. A heavy mist set in, obscuring their vision beyond the immediate few yards in front of them. Nevertheless, they went on, following the tracks that, for the most part, kept to the trail.

"What would you do if the mountain lion came after us?" said Rupert.

"I don't know, consider myself lucky, I guess," said Sandy.

"What do you mean? You're supposed to stand your ground and make noise, even fight if necessary. Though I'd probably just run."

"I wouldn't fight, or even run. I would simply let it eat me," said Sandy, and he flung over his shoulder part of a long scarf. The scarf he had knitted all fall and was about as long as he was. He had no talent for knitting. The scarf was not uniformly shaped, it was wide in parts, slender in others, and had the appearance of undulating waves. There were also numerous small holes. It was Sandy's prized possession.

"Why? Come on, you don't want to die like that, being eaten by some beast at the ripe age of 18."

"I would be an ecological hero. I would fulfill some real purpose, not whatever bullshit consumer ideal they make you believe here at school. You know, I would welcome that death. I hope this thing eats us tonight and poops us out tomorrow. It'd be much worse to live some suburban fantasy and die an old fat ass. You know, they pump your corpse so full of chemicals now you don't even decompose, or hardly... I think it's much more noble to be cat shit."

Rupert believed Sandy. As always, Sandy was very compelling, for he possessed the strength of conviction. Rupert's own words were clumsy in comparison and lacked confidence, nor did he ever fully think through what he said. Sandy, by contrast, gave himself completely and earnestly to the words that he spoke, in a way that made Rupert feel envious. Sandy's speech came across as aware of itself, articulate, and heavily steeped in logic. Rupert both admired and hated him for it, since it caused Rupert to feel slightly inferior. And as is natural for anyone who feels inferior, Rupert was therefore ever-critical of Sandy. His biggest complaint was that he suspected an absence of experience to back half of what Sandy ever said. Rupert thus often found Sandy to be overly opinionated and was frequently irritated by his pontifications. Even so, Rupert liked Sandy and thought him brave.

The temperature dropped and the bitter cold mysteriously commanded a silence between Rupert and Sandy. The mist began to crystalize and shine as brief sparkles in the light of their plastic torch, like silver aspen leaves flickering in a distant summer wind. Rupert noticed his breath linger as steam clouding around him, mingling with the foggy ether. The snow had hardened and crunched beneath their steps. Rupert feared this noise might give away their presence to the animal, though there existed no stated objective as to what they were actually doing. Then the tracks stopped.

"The tracks—"

"Shh!" said Sandy, holding up a hand and furrowing his brow.

Rupert listened but heard nothing. A gust blew and broke his concentration. He became mesmerized by the illumined mist that danced in the wind like ghostly hands beckoning them further into the forest. Then at once the breeze died and all became deathly still, stagnant. Rupert felt a tension, a primeval tension that inexplicably stifled his breath, as if the woods were a sweltering jungle, frigid though it was.

"Maybe we should—" Rupert was immediately interrupted by a low sustained groan, gradually building in volume and intensity yet without a clear point of origin, as if issuing from another world. Once it had reached its peak, the sound came crashing down upon itself in a distorted wailing crescendo. Rupert had paused somewhere between his fear and bewilderment. With extraordinary effort he turned to look for Sandy but all that he saw was a wisp of Sandy's scarf vanishing into the fog, and with him their flashlight. In that second, an impetus for survival moved Rupert to run, bolting into the misty void. The heat he had felt before stayed with him, dripping down his forehead and burning his face, though he paid no mind to it. He was detached from all feeling, even panic. He knew only to run and he could not stop running, blindly retracing their steps back to the dorm with automatic abandon, outside of time.

After some untold distance, his trance was broken by the glow of a streetlamp sifting through the trees, and near it he noticed

Sandy frantically lifting himself up from having slid in his flight. Rupert called to him but Sandy kept moving toward the orange halo. Rupert was reunited with Sandy, but only after he had made it back to their dorm room. It was tacitly understood between them not to talk about what had just happened.

Rusty barked at a squirrel and woke Rupert from his dream of the past. Sandy was no longer consequential to Rupert. His image had returned to a photo in Rupert's dusty high school yearbook, hidden away in the attic. Sandy's photo would no doubt appear ridiculous now, Rupert thought. He had begun to view the things of humanity as ever-becoming inconsequential and ridiculous. Eventually everything would degrade into a state of simple refuse, Rupert mused, like a kitsch souvenir that loses not only its charm but its sentimentality, destined from the start for the landfill. Rupert's yearbook would soon become trash. The Cyclone Dragon, even, would turn someday into a piece of garbage. Rupert found that thought oddly comforting: he liked the idea of being thrown into a landfill, to be crushed into a great sea of compacted rubbish and then dissolved slowly overtime, like spilling into a boundless abyss. There was freedom in this fantasy. Rupert could think of nothing more restricting than a fated coffin, a sealed box. Moreover, Margaret would probably not want to pay for an extra wide casket to hold the vacuum. And there Rupert dropped the subject from his mind.

Rupert's attention turned instead to his son. John had been talking during most of their walk and Rupert had just become aware of his mental absence in their conversation. Rupert had responded to John with an intermittent "yeah" or "uh-huh," though he had not been listening. He had only paid enough attention to know that John was telling what was supposed to be a funny story, and Rupert chuckled automatically whenever John laughed. Rupert felt badly about it. Perhaps he did not speak enough to his son, he thought. He could not recall any real talk between them that he would consider special. Rupert realized then that it had been years since he had hugged John without it being an empty and routine set of choreography, with John agitated and squirming half the time. Rupert made a plan to genuinely hug John, to withhold nothing, and experience authentic tenderness with his son. And yet, Rupert knew that he might never hug either of his children ever again, nor watch them grow. He wanted to tell John how he felt but no words could escape him.

While Rupert and John were out, Margaret arranged to meet with Grundle. By a stroke of tremendous luck, Margaret had set up a time with the lawyer the very next day—what Grundle's secretary called a "miracle" (an abrupt cancellation freed an hour for Grundle in the afternoon). Margaret excitedly shared this news the instant Rupert and John returned from walking the dog. Unwittingly, it was the first moment either Margaret or Rupert had spoken of the matter in front of their children. John at once enquired, and Elsa rushed in from the next room to investigate. Margaret quickly yielded to their line of questioning, giving in softly, warmly. She thought that maybe she had subconsciously meant to bring it all out into the open, that she could not have kept her dear hopes from their children any longer. Margaret revealed everything to them. She illustrated a wondrous and propitious future, making extravagant promises about various items they were to buy. One such item that Margaret was particularly keen on was a boat for the lake they frequented during the summer, the kind of boat they used to watch as a family from the pier and fantasize about owning one day. The children smiled, their eyes became bright, their faces full of confident happiness and genuine enthusiasm. Tears of joy trickled down Margaret's face.

"Mom, can I bring Dad to school tomorrow?" said John.

"Of course, but what for?" said Margaret, kneeling to be eye level with John.

"It's a show and tell day," said John. "I was going to bring my Venus flytrap, but it died."

"Oh, of course you can sweetie," Margaret ran her fingers through John's hair as she spoke. "And then afterwards your father and I will head straight to the lawyer, that enchanter who will make all our dreams come true."

"Yes!" said John. "I'm going to be so popular!"

The next morning Margaret brought Rupert to John's class. Margaret explained to John's teacher, Ms. Page, the situation for his show and tell. Ms. Page laughed with an incredulous tone, automatically assuming Margaret's story was some kind of gag. Then, out of the Dragon, came the voice of Rupert, introducing himself. He sounded (as he always did since the Dragon had swallowed him) like someone speaking from inside a very small space, muffled yet clear. Ms. Page was visibly shocked though she was careful not to express fear. Rather, she searched in vain for an adequate response, stumbling over her words, then fell into a state of silent befuddlement. Even as the bell rang for class to begin, Ms. Page could not break from her seemingly catatonic state, her eyes fixed on someplace far away.

Margaret smiled and took the opportunity to address the children, announcing John's show and tell. John strutted proudly to the front of class with the Dragon by his side.

"This vacuum is no ordinary vacuum," said John. "It can suck up anything in your house, lightning-fast. Carrots—boom! Tennis balls—boom! Remote controls—boom! Cats—boom! Dogs—boom! And people—boom boom boom!"

"No it can't!" said a student.

"Can too, it sucked up my dad—boom!" The class broke into roaring laughter. "Dad! Talk to them!"

"Hi class, I am John's dad, Rupert. It's so very nice to meet you." The laughter ceased and all the class rushed to the vacuum, poking and prodding in inspection. "Watch out kids! You don't want to hit the wrong lever, or you just might wind up in here with me."

The students who were touching the Dragon recoiled instantly. Rupert chuckled. One child burst into tears and ran out of the classroom.

"Don't scare the children Rupert!" said Margaret.

"My dad is going to sue the vacuum people and make us super rich. Boom!" said John. "We're going to live in a big mansion, bigger than any of your houses, the biggest house you've ever seen, because I have a vacuum dad and you don't. Boom!"

The class became a clamoring ruckus. The students swarmed around John in a frenzy that supported him. John held his head regally, as if he were looking down onto the masses from far above. Margaret and Rupert then left, both swelled with an immense sense of pride as parents.

Margaret adeptly hoisted Rupert into their car with the well-practiced technique of using her hip as a sort of fulcrum. She turned on the radio and drove en route to the lawyer's office. An obnoxious commercial break caused Margaret to tune the radio to a different station (from the usual classic rock) and by accident came upon the public programming her grandmother once listened to daily. It had been years since Margaret had listened to this station, or even thought of it. On the air was the show *Divas,* paying tribute that day to the opera great Maria Callas, on her birthday. A phone-in requested to hear the aria "É Strano," from the opera *La Traviata.* As it began to play, Rupert scoffed.

"Oh jeez," said Rupert.

"What?" said Margaret.

"This song is so damn annoying," said Rupert.

"I think it's pretty," said Margaret.

"I can't with this opera, it's far too ahhhhh-ahhhhh," said Rupert, mocking the vocal prowess of the great diva, though muffled by the Dragon. The exertion kicked up residual dust in the vacuum and he coughed a little.

"I like the melody." The aria came to its most majestic moment, commanding a brief pause in the conversation. "Besides, this is Maria Callas," said Margaret.

"So, what's next then, Ave Myself?" Rupert let out a little smug laughter at his far-reaching pun.

Margaret thought of "É Strano" for the first time in twenty years. Effusive tears poured down her face, despite her greatest efforts to hold them back. She did not, however, sniffle or weep audibly—she wished to protect her feelings from Rupert's insensitive remarks. All those years ago, Margaret's grandmother had died in a car accident. Margaret, without ever telling anyone, decided then to find out what her grandmother's favorite station had played around the predicted time of her death. It was "É Strano" sung by Maria Callas, very likely the last piece of music she ever heard. On this drive with Rupert, Margaret pictured the crash once more. She imagined what it may have looked like for her grandmother, and all in slow motion. Her mind could not help but choreograph the images of broken metal and glass on impact to the aria as it played in their car. In some way, she knew deep down that they were heading toward a crash of their own—maybe not in a car, maybe not physical, but a crash nonetheless.

And then it was night. Rupert and Margaret were in their bedroom. They had not spoken since their visit with the lawyer. There was a tension—not one that grows and so can break, but a tension that could remain sunk in the doldrums of an impossible rut. They could stay there forever, in this rut; unresolved and swollen with the hurt between them. Margaret would never release them from this tension, it had to be Rupert, though he struggled to push the necessary air over his vocal cords.

"I had no idea, Margaret, please believe me."

The response from Margaret was a heavy silence. She felt this silence in the pit of her stomach, a peculiar nausea—she held onto this sick sensation as something that affirmed life for her, she could feel nothing else. Her emotions hibernated in a frozen torpor at the bottom of her stomach.

"Margaret? Please believe me, please believe me, I didn't realize, how was I supposed to know? I am a victim, like you said, we just have to find a lawyer who understands vacuums—"

"It's hopeless."

"What?"

"It's hopeless Rupert, no one is going to tell us anything different. As always, we lost, we lost, and we're going to keep on losing... I don't know how we're going to tell the children. John was so proud, we let him down."

"No, we didn't, we're not going to give up, it's just going to take a little more time. We didn't lose. We're not going to let John down, we're not letting anyone down."

"No Rupert, we just have to face the fact that we're losers."

"No baby, never, I won't let that happen, I intend to keep on fighting, for everyone... I wish I could hold you right now and make you feel like everything's going to be alright."

"Don't touch me! Don't you dare... You know what Rupert, you're right, *we're* not losers, *you* are! You and you alone. I should have known, I should have known you'd ruin this. You always act like such an expert, the big man around the house, when you can hardly nail a picture to the wall. Of course you'd throw away the warranty tag, the tag with big bold red letters warning to never remove it, you fucking idiot! You can't even fucking read!"

"So, you do blame me? I thought you said you didn't blame me for any of this?"

"I don't blame you Rupert, I loathe you."

"Please baby, it's not fair, I'm trapped in the dark, I can't move, I—"

"So that's how you're going to respond? It's still all about you isn't it? You and your damn vacuum, no one else matters. I'm tired of being neglected by you, of this whole family being neglected by you."

"I want to change, I want to make everything better. I promise, I just had an accident, it's not as if I'm an alcoholic or something—"

"This is worse, your neglect is worse, I'd rather you were an alcoholic. I could understand if you were an alcoholic, but your addiction is far more insidious, you're addicted to yourself, you don't even need a substance."

"Darling, please don't loathe me, I'm trying, I really am, I'm sorry, I'm sorry for everything."

"You see? You only care about being loathed, not how your behavior affects your family... I don't know if I can do this anymore Rupert."

"Please don't leave me, I love you, I'll make it work, I'll keep on fighting, I'll find another lawyer."

"How? Because I'm not going to look for another lawyer. I'm done with this game, this stupid game of yours."

"I'll find a way."

"Oh, and you're going to tell the children, not me."

"OK, but give me some time, I need some time—"

"I'm not giving you much of anything anymore, I've given everything I can, that's it, I'm tired of always being the one who has to make accommodations for you, compromises for you, do everything on your terms. I'm through with making sacrifices—If you don't tell them by the beginning of next week we are over."

The next week was in just a couple days, the day after John's big game. Rupert attended the game with his family. He listened to the sounds of the referee's whistle, the screech of shoes on the gymnasium floor, the shouts from enthusiastic parents, and all the while he played in his mind the logistics of what should be his own next move, how he might save their dreams. Then a thought came to him: he realized that he could in fact preserve his family's ambitions, though at the forfeit of his own. Margaret had made such sacrifices, he thought, and now he must repay her with his own great sacrifice. His only consolation would be to not have to tell the children about his blunder. He would not have to disappoint them (that, at least, he could escape), if only he dared to...

Rupert had remembered reading about a "Dragon Breath" function that could dissolve (or maybe incinerate, he was not sure) the contents of the vacuum if it ever became clogged. If he were to find and engage this function it would most surely be the end of him. His death his family could easily benefit from since, unbeknownst to Margaret, Rupert had an excellent life insurance policy, one that even covered so-called "freak accidents," and no doubt a causality of the Dragon would qualify. He told himself he would sleep on it.

The following morning Margaret spoke to Rupert for the first time since their argument. (Rupert had since made a few attempts, remarks that either flat out ignored what had transpired between them or laboriously recognized their issue—he would ramble on without any response from Margaret yet desperately act as if she was nevertheless engaged in conversation with him). Margaret on this day, however, broke her silence in order to curtly remind Rupert of his promise to tell the children. Rupert asked if he could break the news to them after their planned dinner at Meat o' Balls (in celebration of John's big game), though Margaret denied his request. Rupert begged, breaking into tears, and Margaret reluctantly conceded, though on the condition only that he stay home during dinner: "no promise, no dinner, and no Meat o' Balls."

Rupert complained that he was being treated like a child, to which Margaret replied: "if the shoe fits" and walked off. Margaret felt an emotional twinge as she walked away, like a psychic paper cut caused by her sharp severity toward Rupert. She knew that her attitude was harsh. And she knew that this harshness gave her pain also, because she still cared for Rupert. But it was necessary, for without this severe approach she would fall into a deep dark well, a place she had been to before and promised she would never return. Her anger at Rupert was the only barrier to falling once again into that debilitating despair.

It was following the birth of her first child, Elsa, when Margaret became familiarized with her black well. Margaret suffered then from an extreme form of a condition known as *postpartum depression.* Margaret could hardly recall the first few months after Elsa's birth, they were so saturated by the well. She became absolutely listless, gave up nursing her infant, could not even bear to be in her child's presence, and was hardly able to eat without throwing up. She looked at life like it was shimmering up above the surface of the well water, ever higher and dimmer with each passing day. Margaret stopped seeing colors, she could not taste, she never heard pleasant sounds or words from others, and she could no longer stand her own scent (which became overpowering to all other smells).

Margaret scarcely noticed Rupert in those days and thought him to be of little help. Rupert had initially reacted to her depression with incredulity and made dismissive, almost flippant comments that sank Margaret even deeper. Only after Margaret's mother moved in to help did Rupert begin to take the matter seriously. He then tried his best with frequent pep talks (that turned into speeches), foot rubs, house chores, and extra parenting. Rupert's attempts seemed to Margaret's mother, however, to be "too little too late"— she blamed him for her daughter's state and vowed never to forgive him (and she never did). Margaret, on the other hand, simply did not notice Rupert, nor even her mother. She was incapable of paying attention to anyone, least of all her infant child.

Margaret, of course, did eventually rise to the top of her well and crawled out, though it took many months. Rupert attributed her triumph to his own valiant efforts of support. Margaret's mother assumed credit as well and chalked up Margaret's recovery to her own exceptional skills as a mother and grandmother. Margaret had convinced herself that it was her love for Elsa that shone through and pulled her out, as well as her desire to be strong for her child. In truth, however, Margaret felt better only because of time. It simply took time.

On the drive to Meat o' Balls, Margaret noticed that the children seemed to relax without the presence of their father. She guessed it was because they could monopolize their mother's attention—obvious conclusions about Rupert she chose to ignore, she had thought of him enough lately. Elsa and John played a game in the back seat, hitting each other in the arm whenever they saw a "slug-bug" Volkswagen. They giggled after every punch. Margaret smiled while she looked at them strike each other in the mirror. She realized that she could not remember the last time the children had laughed together.

Rupert forgot which room of the house he was in. He had formed the habit of imagining the room he was in at all times—he had become quite good at it, so much so that he often forgot he could no longer see. Yet after he heard Margaret and the children walk out the front door, it was as if they had switched off the lights as they left. He was in darkness once more, lost in his own home, and resting in a state of torpid solitude. It was just as well, he thought, now he could go through with his plan.

Rusty found Rupert and came to him whining. Rusty grabbed the cord to the Dragon and pulled, trotting toward the front door. Rupert followed him with his motorized wheels and realized quickly what Rusty needed. The obstacle was the front door, and

Rupert could not open it. He felt sorry for the dog who whined and panted loudly.

"I've let you down too, haven't I?" Rupert said. He heard a loud bark from Rusty, followed by a series of frantic scratches at the door. Then, to Rupert's great surprise, there was the sound of the door swinging open. Somehow, Rusty had done it. Still with the cord in his jaws, he bolted out onto the sidewalk, tugging Rupert close behind him. Rupert's imaginative sight came back into focus: he saw the sidewalk, the trees in front of the houses, the route he and Rusty would always take.

A half hour into their walk, Rusty stopped abruptly at a fork. Rupert always chose the road on the right, flanked by overgrown blackberry bushes along a ditch on one side, and large oak trees in front of grand old houses on the other. It was the historic neighborhood prior to recent developments that cut into surrounding farmland, paving over everything. Rupert liked to imagine what life was like just twenty years before they had moved there, how the landscape had changed. There used to be a patch of remaining farmland that he and Rusty would walk by, where he would try and picture an entire vista of agricultural fields and woodlands. In the last few years, however, those farms too had disappeared, covered up by subdivisions.

Rusty pulled Rupert to the left. Rupert had no clear image of this road and so his vision once again started to fade. The road went down a gentle slope and Rusty kept going down it, down,

down, down—the sensation of descent frightened Rupert but he was at the same time compelled and did not resist. Eventually the sidewalk leveled, and almost as soon as it did Rusty stopped. There were no traffic sounds, no children playing, no distant chatter, no leaf blowers. There was only a silence that gently yielded to the rush of water. Rupert conjured in his mind the primordial crash of waves on rocks by the coast, the hush of foamy seawater passing over sand. He took this fantasy one step further and thought of a salty breeze, of seagulls, of a seemingly eternal watery horizon on fire with the orange of a setting sun.

In fact, Rupert and Rusty were nowhere near the beach. Rather, they rested by an overflowing gutter that gushed into a ditch. Rusty sat motionless, captivated by the rush of the brown water. He dropped the cord to the Dragon from his mouth and whined with a quiet raspy voice. Rupert then heard Rusty walk away. His nails, long overdue for a clipping, scraped on the sidewalk as he trotted. Rupert wanted to call out to him but could not muster the strength to do so. Rupert had only so much strength left in him, and he was going to need all of it.

Rupert grappled with minute movements to find the Dragon Breath function. As he toiled, a young sounding man who was accompanied by at least one other person (a young woman as far as Rupert could tell) approached the Dragon.

"Woah, nice vacuum," said the young woman.

"Yeah, so nice it belongs in the ditch," said the young man, who grabbed the Dragon's handle. "Damn, what's in this?" he said, struggling with all his might to lift the vacuum.

"Let go of me, leave me alone," said Rupert.

The young man dropped Rupert (from the eight or so centimeters he was able to lift him) and screamed. Rupert heard frantic footsteps scurry away and he was soon by himself again. By luck, being dropped jostled Rupert just enough to land a finger (or perhaps a toe) on a lever that he did not know was there. By process of elimination, he deduced that it must be for the Dragon Breath function. He switched it on unceremoniously and without hesitation. He felt a warm liquid pass over him and guessed that it was his last moment without intense pain. His first thought to fill this moment was about Elsa, about how beautiful she was as a baby and how adorable she was as a small child. He remembered one summer: Margaret was six months pregnant with John and they had just bought a new bed to help with her back pain. Rupert placed the old mattress in the backyard and left it there for about a month before taking it to the transfer station. During those weeks, Rupert and Elsa would lay on the old mattress and look at the stars together. Sometimes he would read bedtime stories to her by flashlight on the mattress.

Rupert realized that these musings over the past had lasted longer than he expected. The warm liquid had cooled and he had become uncomfortable but was in no real pain. He tried pushing the lever further to one side, and then switched it off and on again. Still, nothing. It then struck Rupert that he had made an error. The Dragon Breath function required a special fluid that did not come with the vacuum, it had to be ordered separately. The warm liquid he felt must have been his own urine—the lint chamber was backed up, no doubt.

Rupert wheeled the Dragon back up the slope, retracing his "steps." He would have to face his family. He would have to give them nothing. Halfway up the incline, he heard the sounds of the motor wane. Then the wheels stopped. He rolled back slightly. "Must be a dead battery," he thought.

INTERMISSION

I have become overwhelmed by emotion from reading Joe's journals, the scrambled writings from which I have given myself the enormous task of transcribing into a cohesive tale. It is for my own solace and inner clarity that I must take this moment now to recount, briefly, my introduction to this universe, the door that Joe opened for me. I had never heard of people being swallowed by vacuums and I must confess as to my initial skepticism; the idea was reminiscent of an old time sailor spinning his yarn about men living in the bellies of sea monsters. However, while the so-called sea monsters of yore are simply known today as whales, we do not yet know what these vacuums might become. It is even possible (though my research has failed to confirm its existence) this vacuum monster might be exactly as it is described by Joe. Perhaps the vacuum has been buried by those who wish it to be unknown, by companies that could face financial loss if the dangers of the vacuum are made public—surely not every scandal survives the corporate fossil record.

I arrived a few minutes late, 11:03 PM. The house was situated on a busy corner, though sheltered in the quietude of its age—hidden behind large red cedars that drooped their boughs over a frost-bitten lawn. I walked over the crumpling grass that led to the veranda. The ground relieved my feet and slowed the moment like a soft parachute. A frigid mist held still in the air, and all the snails that once crept in secret perambulations were dead in winter. No one missed these snails, but I did. The life cycle of the snail rested beneath the dead garden bramble, as did the spiders and insects, like chthonic spirits that whispered to me.

I was met at the door by members of Joe's family. I was to spend the night caring for my elderly friend, who was dying. His grandson showed me what to do: how to operate his mechanical bed, how to administer the morphine, give him water, and so on. Gracefully he held his grandfather's hand and kissed his forehead, wishing him "goodnight" as if it were his last, and it very nearly was. Then they were gone, all but his wife who slept upstairs. Otherwise, it was just Joe and me, resting in the evening warmth of the old house.

Joe was 92 years young. He had been active and healthy his entire life, even in advanced age, and only in the last couple of months had that changed. I noticed that night that even in his twilight hours he was handsome: mustached, strong jawed, possessing an intelligent and elegant face. He had been robust most his life; he scaled half a dozen peaks over 3000 meters in his 65th year. He was also a fine sculptor, his primary medium clay: mostly either abstract pieces (emitting a serene yet sensual aura) or figures honoring motherhood—his career was that of a GP and he had delivered hundreds of infants in his time. Now this man, who had helped bring so much life into the world, was ready to leave it. I was saddened but honored to be in his presence that night.

Joe was just barely communicative. We spoke briefly about mountaineering. Or rather, I spoke and he gave one-word responses. I asked him what it was like at the crater of a 4000 meter mountain in our area. He lacked the strength to answer, though raised his brow in silent reverie. He joked that he would answer my questions two at a time (I think I get that joke). I didn't press him further but instead retold a story of my father's who had climbed a similar-sized mountain and found at its peak a swarm of thousands of orange butterflies. Joe smiled, bemused, and exclaimed an approving "wow."

Joe winced in pain. I held his hand to comfort him for several minutes. His hand was cold yet exuded a warmth of character. He seemed to need this contact in these final moments, he would not let go of this life. The news was playing constantly in the background and it was clear that he intended to remain connected to the world (though, according to his pain, death could not come sooner). He did not wish to say goodbye, instead he wanted to pass while still part of this world.

He slept, so I helped myself to the snacks his family left for me in the fridge. I walked slowly and pensively through the house. The hardwood floor creaked loudly under my feet. Even though I had been in those rooms dozens of times prior, everything appeared different. I noticed subtle details that gave the house a somewhat surreal quality: a stuffed penguin peeked between pots stored atop an armoire, a small carnival mask with peacock feathers hung over the entry to the kitchen, a dim filament bulb swayed gently from side to side though there was no breeze, mail was strewn across an oak wood table next to the morphine. Joe's oxygen tank was loud, rhythmic, but somehow soothing. A small beetle held onto the side of an indoor plant and appeared in that moment like a savage wild animal. There was a certain glow that lingered throughout, a hazy golden presence that was tangible but not visible. The atmosphere was peaceful, so much so that what little sleep I did manage on the couch provided me with a deep sense of rest.

Joe's wife woke me a little past 6 AM and shortly thereafter I departed. I returned later to spend another night at Joe's place, but by then he was not truly conscious. He would not talk, drink water, nor even open his eyes. He sometimes held an arm to his forehead or tugged at the bars near the side of his bed. I tried my best to make him comfortable: frequently reconfiguring his pillows or massaging his shoulders. His eyes constantly watered, or perhaps they were tears from the pain. I left around the same time the next morning and a few hours later Joe's wife called to tell me he was dead.

A few months after his death, Joe's wife offered to give me one of his sculptures. It is partially unfinished (I am unfamiliar with the ceramic process but I think it is lacking a kind of glaze on one side) though one would never notice from most angles. When standing, it is level with my hip and has a sensuous figure-eight shape to it—an obvious symbol of infinity I smiled at when I first saw it. The sculpture was too heavy for Joe's wife to move, laying on its side in a wooden crate up in the attic. I awkwardly finessed the crate out of the small attic door, down narrow stairs, and schlepped it home. When unpacking the sculpture, a great plume of clay-dust emanated from the box like the opening of an ancient Egyptian sarcophagus. Once I had the sculpture out, I had the good sense to rummage through the packing material for anything else of importance, and that was where I discovered fragments of his journals, hidden for decades under an old unfinished sculpture. Of course, I plan to return the journals to his family, who would no doubt want them, but only after I have finished my writing, as selfish as that may be.

I believe it necessary to the telling of this story, as well as only fair to Joe as a source, to include his own introduction to the vacuum tale. Below are selected excerpts from his journal:

It is strange how I have managed to avoid the mountains all these years. And yet, now that I am finally here, I am struck by a peculiar sort of familiarity echoing through these sheer alpine slopes. I would not say "déjà vu," it is not the sensation of having been here before. Rather, I feel as though I have always been here, and that the life I have lived until now, away from these peaks, was nothing more than a dream. That is not to say I believe in any kind of mysticism—déjà vu and the like are merely psychological phenomena originating in the brain. However, there is a particular presence here one can not deny and causes me to understand why so many of the more primitive alpine villages are prone to intense superstition...

Today I set myself up in a charming little guesthouse situated in a green little valley in the shadow of Monk peak. I am of course pleased that the conference is to be held here, in this village untainted by the modern world. However, I hardly see why this particular locale was necessary, fascinating though it is. I suppose it is merely an excuse for the board to be on holiday. I too was rather hoping, having arrived a couple days prior to the event, to avail myself of some thoughtful solitude in appreciation of nature—to see what restorative wonders the clean mountain air could give my tired city mind. I am sorry to say, however, that my simple plan for tranquil recreation has been thwarted, by an uncouth neanderthal from Frankfurt who fancies himself a psychiatrist. He recognized me from who-knows-where and drew me into his clutches, seating me at his luncheon table—which laboriously transformed into dinner, followed by a "night cap," as he put it. At 11:15 PM I have only just escaped. Still, my experience with the man was so odd that I am compelled to recount some piece of it for my own amusement later...

The psychiatrist calls himself Joff, Dr. Herman Joff, and he was accompanied by the strangest creature I have ever met. The creature, I am told, is Dr. Joff's own offspring. As two humans can only produce another human, by the fundamental laws of nature, it is only good sense to assume that the creature is human. Indeed, I could not help but refer to his offspring as a human, a son. I was quickly corrected.

"Species is an arbitrary distinction, is it not doctor?" Dr. Joff told me, as the oily juices of his bratwurst spurted haphazardly from underneath his enormous white mustache.

"No, I'm not sure what you mean. Are you to tell me that your son is somehow not human or is it that you undermine the entire field of taxonomy?"

I had no intention to be humorous, yet Dr. Joff laughed like a volcanic eruption. Bits of sauerkraut sputtered across our table.

"It is always a construct, doctor, a social arbitration. Does the nutcracker fly around calling itself a nutcracker? No, it is we who label it as such, and if we were to instead call it a blue-tit the animal would nevertheless remain the same!"

"Sure, but we make these distinctions in order to make sense of our world, and each distinction is particular, it does not repeat itself— we do not call the nutcracker a nutcracker one day and a blue-tit the other because there is a different animal that we call a blue-tit, and there can only be one blue-tit. To make things even more clear we have developed taxonomy to surpass our colloquialisms—the blue-tit in fact is no longer the blue-tit but Cyanistes caeruleus—"

"I see you know your birds my dear fellow!" Dr. Joff bellowed, seemingly unfazed by my remark. *"But they are categories, semantics—a rose by any other name!"*

"I acknowledge your point Dr. Joff but I must insist that these semantics, as you say, are necessary to the development of language. Without them we would not be having this conversation, nor any conversation."

"Fiddlesticks—we must broaden our minds doctor if we are to call ourselves men of science, and look beyond our societal

conditionings. My offspring is my grand achievement in this exploration into the unknown. My offspring is one of a kind, a completely new individual—by name Googaroo, as it calls itself, the first individual who branded itself with a name, under no other influence than its own will to assert itself—"

"Googaroo-oo-ooooo!" The creature howled.

I looked at Googaroo for a moment, until my befuddled stare was broken by a wide-eyed grunt and slight lunge in my direction, presumably a threat. I looked back at Dr. Joff. "Are you suggesting?—"

"Yes! That Googaroo is without species, without most of the societal chains that bind us. Googaroo is our hope doctor, our desperate plea for liberation, to free the depths of our consciousness!"

"And it is Googaroo, then, that you are presenting at the conference?"

"Correct doctor." Googaroo leapt from its chair and ran (switching back and forth between bipedal and quadrupedal styles of locomotion). "There it goes doctor! See how it acts on impulse!"

"Is he always like this around cats?" I asked.

"For a while, at first, it made associations with the neighborhood cats. Then Googaroo became very attached to pigeons and would perch above the kitchen sink to sleep at night. And now Googaroo is most bonded with our dog—Zandi."

"What about language acquisition? Does Googaroo say 'Zandi' ever, for instance?"

"Trust me doctor, Googaroo is extraordinarily articulate. Googaroo has a gift for gab, as you people say, and a delightful repartee in conversation—though not according to polite society. Googaroo rather possesses a free and spontaneous form of communication that is not bound to the restrictive principles of what so-called 'language' must be."

"What does this sound like?"

"'What does this sound like'? My dear doctor, what does this look like, what does this smell like, what does this taste like?—there are more aspects to communication than we account for in our daily lives. The bear in estrus will leave scent markings for the male bear to locate her and copulate—is this not communication?"

"Does Googaroo scent mark?"

"Yes! Googaroo has recently begun scent marking, in this 19th year of Googaroo's life. It is my conviction that Googaroo is now looking for a mate, though I must continue to analyze the urine and droppings to be sure—these are not yet findings I will be presenting at the conference and must ask you not to repeat what I am telling you here in confidence."

"Oh yes, of course—there's Googaroo coming back now! What does he have in his hands, mud?"

"Not mud, most likely droppings, a typical medium for communication—there are many sculpted shapes in Googaroo's repertoire—if Googaroo spits on a conical mound Googaroo has discovered a new animal in the bushes over there."

"Dear lord, does Googaroo not have any sense of hygiene?"

"A question that is most typical of your profession doctor! Yes, Googaroo has an innate conception of hygiene—when I place peanuts (Googaroo's preferred food) on the droppings Googaroo will usually not eat the peanut! Is that not astounding doctor? Here you have an animal that has never been taught hygiene and yet will practice it—perhaps this may provide insight into the roots of

hygiene in our collective psyche, maybe even the evolution of hygiene as we know it!"

The discussion from this point onwards stepped over my curious mind and began to simply repulse me. I could not, however, bring myself to leave their company. I was frozen by my own shock in dealing with the mad man and his creation. When at long last I remembered my right to liberty and rose from (what had been) lunch's table to excuse myself, Dr. Joff became relentless with his invitation to dinner... It is with a weary mind now that I retire for the night...

I nearly forgot—I also must note before bed that I wish for tomorrow to not only escape the Joffs and explore on my own but to investigate: the creature, as he ran from the bushes, brought to my attention a man near to there, by a stream, who seemed quite disturbed by Googaroo and was waiving a broom vehemently in his direction, undoubtedly and justifiably for self-protection. The scene appeared odd, however (beyond the obvious with Dr. Joff's abomination to humanity), and I can't help but think that the man is unwell in some way. There seemed to be an encampment, so perhaps he lives by that stream. By oath I must inquire...

The villagers advised against my meeting with this mystery man by the stream. Of course they had my personal safety in mind, yet from the perspective only of superstition—they believe him to be something like a warlock since he is often seen gesticulating wildly with a broom. I, however, possessing zero fears of supernatural forces (I do not believe in such hogwash) made my call to the man who seemed yesterday to be in a state of psychological distress (mental health may not be my focus as a GP though I know of nearby institutions that could help)—it is a shame to see someone in a place as naturally beautiful as this suffer so! And why? Because antiquated superstition prevents any local from helping the man.

The man is clearly older but it is difficult to guess his exact age—a short white beard, bald head, sun-tanned skin, glasses, wearing an orange robe like a monk. With his broom he was sweeping around a vacuum chained to a concrete slab, positioned like some sort of altar piece. His silent task of sweeping had a serene quality, and when he seemed to finish he laid with his broom at the foot of the vacuum altar with tranquil requiescence. I did not wish to disturb him, though it was obvious to me that he required help.

My approach thankfully did not startle the man. When I announced my presence he simply opened his eyes without the slightest change in expression on his relaxed face. I asked his name, why he was camping there, if he was hungry or sick, and if he felt he needed anything. I also asked about his family. He did not respond to a single question, only lay staring. There was a seemingly eternal period of complete silence following my line of questions and I felt for a moment as though I was stepping too far outside of my professional comfort zone. I assured him that I was a doctor, to which he smiled.

"Come back tomorrow evening, when the clock tower strikes nine, and I will tell you my story," he said.

I nodded and said "thank you," though I am unsure as to what I was thankful for. I left with an exhilarating sense of adventure before me that persists to now. I am anxious to get through the first day of the conference and to meet this mysterious person once again.

I found the man, to my great astonishment, dressed in a suit and tie, laying as he was when I had left him. He propped himself up with his broom and made a quiet beckoning gesture with his hand. No words passed between us—silently he brought me to his tarpaulin hut where beside it was a wicker table and two chairs. A bottle of Don Perignon with two crystal glasses was set by candlelight. The moon was rising, illuminating the young trees and bushes on the banks of the stream like some enchanted forest.

We did not toast but drank languidly in the amber and silver glow of it all, without a single utterance from either of us. Whenever my glass became empty he would smile slightly from the left corner of his mouth and serve me. I felt as though he was putting me under some sort of trance—I felt all my cares slip away and could only sense the still evening ambience.

I was thus highly disturbed when the mood suddenly changed. The moment the bottle was (finally) finished, a chilly gust of wind blew violently through the bramble and extinguished our candle. I pulled up my collar to the cold. When my sight adjusted to the softer moonlight I was startled to find the man's wide eyes fixed upon mine. His gaze had an intensity about it that frightened me to the core, and I had no idea what his intentions could possibly be. I scooted my chair back so that I could stand but a thread from my blazer sleeve got stuck in the wicker. I looked down briefly as I ripped my arm loose but in that moment the man had already vanished. I began walking cautiously away, trying not to show any fear, but had not gone more than ten yards before I heard recorded music echoing throughout the place. I looked for the source of the music and then saw the man, glowing with moonlight in a tiny clearing like a ghost, broom   in   hand.

What happened next is impossible to adequately put into words, all I can truly say is that he danced. He danced to an old recording of "É Strano." He moved his broom like an extension of his own body—he was extremely graceful! His movements had a true balletic quality and he wore on his face an ageless expression so beautiful it brought me to tears. I have never seen such emotive depth to movement, nor such elegance, and all punctuated by the haunting aria.

When both he and the music finished, he lay with his broom in the manner I've seen with him before. I could hardly catch my breath, the entire experience was utterly overwhelming. I departed without saying anything, walking through the brief woodland with dried salty tears that stung my eyes in the soft breeze... I must visit with this man once more and truly learn his story—not because I am a doctor (it obviously has nothing to do with that) but because I must know.

—

"Bullshit," said Kurt Bass, and put down the book he was reading on his break. It was a thin mildewy paperback, missing its cover, taken from a "little free library" box in his neighborhood. It was free, so he had picked it up. Kurt was a frugal man. He had a small collection of discarded literature and random sidewalk castaways at home. This book, however, he planned on tossing. He switched to reading the paper, which was delivered to the office daily, so he could read it for free. Kurt Bass was a mattress salesman.

Kurt sipped the complimentary coffee from his office and turned to the obituaries. He searched for the oldest person who had died. He read about a Chinese seamstress who, at 101, died "peacefully" at her home in Chinatown. "Bullshit," he muttered. Then he looked for the most unusual obituary: "Kurt Bass, 59: avid hiker found dead after likely bear attack." For a moment his blood ran cold and his breath became shallow. Then he came to his senses. "Bullshit," Kurt said out loud—*I never hike*, he thought.

After his shift was over, Kurt walked home. Chilly winds swept over the cold Pacific and whistled through narrow spaces between buildings. The chill blasted unsuspecting T-shirted pedestrians with goosebumps and the stench of alleyway garbage. The cold was unseasonable for August, but not too unusual, particularly whenever there was a "marine layer." A damp piece of paper-trash blew from the alley and stuck to Kurt's ankle. He desperately tried to kick it off. The paper moved from his ankle to his shoe, and from his shoe to his knee, and from his knee to his chest. He pinched the corner of the soggy pungent paper and held it, arm outstretched, to let the breeze take it away.

Kurt arrived at his building. The stairs leading to his front door seemed still and ominous. With each step he felt as though he was coming closer to some grotesque and secret truth, as if approaching the mouth of an enormous yet hidden cave. Kurt went to unlock his door, and at that moment he felt a deep vibration that rattled the key between his thumb and index finger. Alarmed, Kurt peeked through the blinds of a window by his door. Though he saw nothing but the fog of his breath on the glass, and the shadowy rug of his living room, he could not help but sense a strange heavy presence, something like a low rumble. Kurt was puzzled as to what he should do. It seemed silly for him to be afraid. He had complained many times before about a washer in the downstairs laundry room that shook the walls whenever it got to its third cycle. He thought that it had been replaced a while ago, but perhaps not. He turned the key and swung the door open with a pretense of confidence.

Kurt found his apartment empty and quiet. Nothing appeared to be different from when he left earlier that morning. As the days were still long, the sun was on high while his apartment lay dingy and shaded below. Kurt closed the door behind him. He lived alone, or nearly did. Kurt had only one friend in the world: a red-eared slider turtle named Richard. He kept Richard in a gigantic terrarium that took up the only available space for a couch in the tiny living room of his one bedroom apartment. Kurt's only furniture was thus a small round table and stool, both of which he found by a dumpster behind his office. His collected flotsam and jetsam of the city streets he either stored in his one closet or stacked by the wall, particularly books and magazines. He also possessed two Persian rugs, which he actually bought (the only luxury items he ever purchased); one for the living room, which was half covered by the terrarium, and one for the miniscule bedroom—truly a *bed*-room since it was scarcely big enough for a bed. Which was just as well. Kurt slept on the floor, in a sleeping bag. He felt pride in having accomplished the irony of not owning a mattress.

Kurt had sold mattresses for over 30 years. Over time, Kurt became more isolated in his lifestyle, and so selling mattresses evolved into the only context by which he was comfortable talking to people. Granted, mattresses essentially sold themselves, so he did not have to be all that personable, and no customer ever approached to get to know *him*, just to know more about mattresses. Kurt had acquired a considerable amount of knowledge about the store's products, and about mattresses in general. Indeed, one of his few delights in life were the opportunities he had to show off his expertise. This behavior in no way helped to sell mattresses, as customers generally had no use for the finer points.

For over ten years Kurt had been the caretaker of Richard, the turtle. And for more than a decade Kurt had felt smug joy in making little snide remarks to Richard, usually meant to guilt trip him. Richard, whose tank was a great palace, complete with waterfalls, ferns, a pool, a log, and flesh tone pebbles—he should know how good he had it compared to Kurt.

"Comfortable, Richard?" Kurt would ask with a sneer. "How's that nice waterbed, Richard?"

Or he would ask: "How's the good life treating you Richard?—oh don't worry about me, Richard, I'll be just fine on the floor tonight."

Or: "You lead a charmed life, Richard, just charmed."

Richard lived in a glass terrarium he could not leave. Actually, Richard was female. Kurt lived in a small apartment he was forced to leave for several hours of the day. Richard liked to stare at the rug from a log in her tank as she sunned herself under the UV bulb. The rug was intricate and mesmerizing, with a beautiful red fillagree around its border. Richard could not see the color red, to her it looked bluish grey, and the pattern appeared fuzzy, yet nevertheless it captivated her on a daily basis.

Kurt would amuse himself with pointless unanswerable questions he often discussed with Richard. For example: "If one of a conjoined twin is found guilty of a crime, say, murder, but the other twin is innocent, how would you go about convicting that guilty twin?—listen up Richard, this affects you too, you don't want to wind up some conjoined twin's turtle soup and let the bastard get away with it, now do you?"

Kurt, who was nearly 60, already spoke with the higher pitch of a bitter old man. Richard was a medium sized young turtle. Red-eared sliders generally only vocalize as chirps and hisses during mating rituals (or to assert dominance/etc.), which Richard was doomed to never engage with due to the confines of her terrarium— forever mute. Kurt was of medium height, pale, and mostly thin. He had recently acquired a small pot-belly because of his overall lack of physical activity. He was clean shaven with the exception of an unattractive pencil mustache. He had white thinning hair, slicked back with the help of some ancient pomade. He wore large spectacles, polo shirts of various neon colors, beige khaki pants or cargo shorts, and white sneakers with close to knee-high white socks. On particularly hot days he donned short-shorts, almost cheeky shorts, exposing his sickly white, gangly, and hairy thighs, yet still with the sneakers and socks pulled all the way up. On cold days he wore a beige trench coat and a brown knitted scarf his mother made him years ago. Richard had no memory of her parents. Kurt was a man only a mother could love.

Richard's shell was dark green and her skin was light green with yellow stripes and red streaks above her ears. Richard was unable to recognize her own image. Kurt, however, could recognize his own image. He sometimes spent over an hour looking at himself in the mirror—it was all part of his shaving ritual. He was not vain, he simply wanted to visualize himself as a tulip bulb.

In the early 17th century, there existed in the Netherlands what later became known as "tulip mania." During these crazed decades, an economic bubble ballooned out of control, inflated by one commodity: tulips. At its zenith, a single bulb of a rare variety could fetch as much as ten times the annual income of a successful tradesman, or about the equivalent of $1,000,000 by Kurt's day. This, of course, was absurd, and reality eventually caught up with the mania. The speculative bubble caused false expectations of exorbitant profit, and so merchants could not look beyond the hype that grossly overestimated the value of tulips. Not only that, but they were buying and selling faster than the actual distribution of the bulbs. Then one day, inexplicably, virtually no buyers showed up at auction. They just simply were not there. Almost over night, the price for bulbs plummeted. Merchants who had invested huge fortunes were suddenly stuck with piles and piles of unplanted bulbs—not even flowers, just bulbs—worth less than the carts they were delivered in. The bulb that was once as good as gold was now just a bulb.

Back then, the tulip was a new and exotic import. In contemporary Netherlands, tulips paint whole fields with bold strokes of color, easily seen from the windows of commuter trains. These glorious rainbows shone bitterly for centuries in the face of the Dutch, forever a bright and cheerful reminder of a bad idea. Kurt saw this charming piece of history as a metaphor for all humanity— really, he was thinking of America. In America you were told as a child that you were special, that you could grow up to "be somebody." A young American with unique abilities was sometimes referred to as a "budding talent." When a person matured into a successful career, it would often accompany the description from others as "blossoming." If this occurred at a later stage than one's peers the person would be called a "late bloomer." If an individual did not ever "blossom" that person would lose all value in American society, unless they were in the act of buying something.

The majority of Americans, in fact, did not blossom. Some would debase at a younger age than others, but it would eventually happen to most. One day you're in college, the next day you're a mattress salesman. And the day after that you're 60. Many among the flowerless would nonetheless overestimate their intrinsic value. Kurt Bass was a man who knew exactly what his value was.

"We're nothing but a bunch of tulip bulbs, Richard, pretending to be gold," Kurt would say. Richard had never pretended to be anything in her life. And she was not valuable at all. Kurt found Richard as a small baby turtle in a plastic terrarium, the kind with a handle to carry home from the pet store. Richard had been left in this carrier on the concrete floor of the interior stairwell in Kurt's apartment building, by the entrance to the second floor. Richard had been left there without food or water, just bare plastic, by Oscar. He was a father who had set down his grocery bag and terrarium so that he could search for his keys in his bottomless coat pockets. Then, his mobile phone buzzed and absent mindedly he picked up the groceries but not the turtle. The turtle he had bought from a 91 year old seamstress in Chinatown for five dollars, meant as a present for his eight year old son, Kaleb. He soon realized that he had left the turtle on the stairs but in the span of five minutes the turtle had been nabbed by Kurt, who told himself the turtle had been abandoned (but knew, deep down, he was stealing). Perhaps Kurt felt a profound need for friendship. Or maybe he saw something of himself in Richard: a worthless creature in a tiny barren box, left alone and scared of what was outside this box, hiding in a shell.

Kurt sighed... it was ridiculous to fear the obituary. It must be a coincidence, or a practical joke—he never hikes. With a sense of relief, Kurt yawned and then thought he would make some coffee, just one cup. Or maybe some black tea instead. He walked to the kitchen, which had no windows and was dark. He flipped on the light and went over to the stove to put on the kettle. At that moment, however, he noticed an overpowering and oddly terrifying scent. It was musky and reeked of Death's fermentation. A second later, the odor was accompanied by a loud grumbling sound, clearly at close proximity. The floor shook beneath him and the ground coffee leapt from his spoon. Kurt could hardly move, but with a trembling body he turned to face whatever it was.

The refrigerator door was wide open and behind it was something moving, a large black mass of some kind. It thrashed the fridge violently and made that bizarre and horrible sound. Kurt froze like a deer in headlights and found it impossible to think or to even breathe. In his nervous state, the muscles in his right hand went limp and the spoon fell on the linoleum, making a loud ping. The commotion near the fridge then stopped suddenly, and it was quiet, but in some way that made the situation even more frightening. Rising to a height well above the refrigerator was everything Kurt feared it was: a tall, massive, snarling bear, with fur as dark as night and even blacker pupils. Its nose and upper lip quivered for a moment, exposing a pair of gleaming maxillary canines, appearing well used and experienced. The atmosphere was hot and swollen with the beast's smell, and Kurt's face seemed to bake in the creature's breath. Kurt thought for a moment that perhaps this furry apparition was merely the product of his mind. If he simply ignored it, it would go away. However, the bear quickly put that thought to rest by ripping the fridge door off its hinges.

Kurt had no living family other than a niece. Actually, she was hardly his niece, she was the daughter of his brother's wife's sister. His brother and sister-in-law, who were both much older than Kurt, never had any kids. They died in their 70s, within a year of each other, not long before Kurt saw the bear. So this "niece" was Kurt's only possible heir. Her name was Betty. She was on a train when Kurt went missing, though it would be a few days until she learned of his death, and that a huge terrarium along with two Persian rugs were all that she inherited, but that was not important. [An investigating officer did not know what to do about the turtle, so she released her into a park pond where Richard met another turtle, and where she found a favorite rock to sun-soak—Richard missed the Persian rug but not Kurt, she hardly knew he existed].

At this moment, Betty was on the train. She was in her sheltered space within, eyes closed to the sun, and all that she saw was red. Richard could not see red but she also liked to bathe in the sun, eyes closed. Betty tried mindful breathing, but as she took in her initial deep breaths she noticed that her heart rate increased (as it often did for a minute before she was able to fully relax). Her pulse had always made her uneasy, she did not like being aware of it, it gave her the feeling that life was fragile. Somewhere out there, beyond her glowing eyelids, she sensed that the sun too had a fragile pulse, encompassed by a cold and empty cosmos. The indifference of the earth with the magma beneath, the absurd flow of the ocean, it all seemed too close to her. To return to a quiet state, she imagined she was on a Dutch train with great swathes of tulips zipping past the window in flashes of brilliant color. The imagery soothed her and she was finally able to relax. However, Betty was not on a train in Holland, she was on a train in Japan.

The date was August 6th, 2025. The time was 8:16 in the morning. At that precise moment, a man who missed the last train home woke up on a park bench outside Hiroshima station. And exactly 80 years prior, the first nuclear bomb was dropped over the city. Yukio, a 71 year old gardener who had put off a trip to Nara by one more day (a plan to reconcile the compunction of a 20 year silence between himself and a son who lived there) was incinerated. The bomb was carried by an American B-29 called the Enola Gay. The bomber's surname was a common word used in 1945 America, which most typically referred to a state of jovial euphoria or happiness. Betty was an American traveling 80 years later, and was completely ignorant of the anniversary, as were most foreigners in Japan that day. She did not know the light she closed her eyes to was not too dissimilar to the light that burned shadows on walls in a flash, like X-rays of the soul. Betty knew only her anxiety, sourced from concurrent waves of nostalgia and regret. She wanted to forget, or at least distract.

A man who had missed the last train home woke up on a park bench. He was an American named Jacob. He was awakened by Japan's summer heat as he lay across the park bench. After rubbing his blurry tired eyes, the first thing he saw that morning was a limping pigeon, hopping along in front of him. It had the plastic piece that holds together a sixpack of beer tangled around its right foot. An old man, who sat on the next bench over, smiled and nodded to Jacob in that special way one does to someone who doesn't speak the same language, and Jacob clearly did not. Jacob had a moment of dreamlike thinking, as he was not yet prepared to think as though he was awake. He saw the pigeon not as a pigeon but as a rare creature, the last of its kind, almost mythical. Or maybe it *was* mythical, like in a fairy tale—caught by an evil spell and doomed to live forever as a pigeon. Perhaps the only way to break the hex was to release it from its ball-and-chain of garbage. And by the same dream-logic, and without hesitation, he lunged for the pigeon. But the bird immediately evaded his clutches and flew out of the park, passing between two apartment buildings, then out of sight. He looked over at the old man who had smiled but the man quickly turned down his head to avoid eye-contact.

Jacob walked a few blocks back to Hiroshima station and caught the next train. He was trying to make his way back to the town he had been living in for over a month. It was a fairly small town, interlaced with quaint little farms and densely wooded hills. Old women sold their garden vegetables out of self-serve boxes by the roadside. A river ran through the town and past the town's only landmark: a small castle on a hill, surrounded by a moat. The town was called Inuyama, which translates to "dog mountain." Jacob missed his dog back home. He had moved to Inuyama out of happenstance.

Jacob enjoyed people-watching on the train, assigning ridiculous names to strangers and coming up with elaborate back stories. He managed to find an empty seat in train car number four, which is an unlucky number in many parts of east Asia, being that it is similar to the Chinese character for death, though Jacob did not know that. Across the aisle from him was another foreigner, a woman with red hair who sat with her eyes closed, basking in the sunlight that beamed through her window.

Jacob tried to guess her story. He gave her the name Angelica Katz. He imagined she was in deep thought because she was on her way to Tokyo to meet her husband, Harry Katz, and was contemplating a divorce. Her husband had bought her the cheapest plane ticket he could find so she had to take an eight hour train ride from an airport nowhere near Tokyo, after traveling all the way from Omaha, Nebraska. Harry Katz had been in Tokyo the last few weeks doing research on a children's book idea of his, what he called "Dr. Seusshi." It was a sequel to a potty training book he called *Morton Hears a Poo* and other "A-plops Fables," meant as a sort of cautionary tale about undercooked foods. He took a loan out on their house to pay for the expense. Angelica had to drop out of nursing school so they could pay for the mortgage. Also in the works was a book of tongue-twisters called *Mother Moose.*

On a trip to Portland, OR, Harry had become entranced by the wide assortment of unusual ice cream flavors at food trucks, and so he decided to try and revolutionize the niche market. It was not enough, in Harry's mind, to simply have cucumber as an unusual flavor, or balsamic vinegar mixed with strawberries. Harry was ready to take the concept to the next level. His first attempt was an ashtray flavor called "grandpa," which he pitched as having an "earthy" aftertaste. He thought of creating a "back of the bus" curd, but Angelica talked him out of it. Another crackpot idea, that failed, was a hotel-pillow-mint flavored ice cream called "one night stand." Angelica wished it would have only been a one night stand between them, if that. She was only 34 years old, had her own ambitions, and was ready to leave. She no longer wanted to support his ludicrous ventures, such as a fart-vent for the bed, accompanied with fart-filtering underwear he called "thunderwear." Not to mention a travel-sized wedge that stopped tables from wobbling but was built with such cheap material that it flattened after just a few uses.

Jacob's focus then shifted to what he could see out the window, past the woman with her eyes closed. He noticed houses, streaking past his field of vision. Jacob disliked tract housing, it gave him a sick feeling in the pit of his stomach. He looked out the window past Angelica's face and saw dozens of new construction projects for tract housing. In some places, the tract housing appeared to be an ocean, their roof tops glistening like sea waves in the sun. At least the roofs in Japan are made of terracotta, he thought—but then followed that thought with the idea that once everything is made to look the same it becomes ugly, terracotta or no terracotta. The sick feeling in the pit of his stomach came down to his lack of control: Jacob could not save the world, and the world was being ravenously devoured by tract housing.

The train slowed to a stop due to an unlucky case of traffic congestion on the rails. As the train came to a halt, a slow vibrating hum reverberated throughout the passenger cabin. The sound gave Jacob an ineffable sense of dread, an old feeling that welled up from an ancient unknown source within, though in some way familiar. Jacob never figured it out, but this mysterious familiarity came from a dream he had at age seven. He was with his mother visiting family in New Zealand, and had just watched a campy film adaptation of *Dracula* on an old black and white television set. Young Jacob then fell asleep, at about the same moment his face touched the pillow of his cushiony bed, as if sleep was a seductive vampire. His dreams were like cotton candy, soft, sweet, ethereal; his rest was cool and comfortable after a hot January day. Then he had what could only be described as a nightmare. He saw a boundless color of jaundice, though compressed, flat, and infinitely bound in its dimension. Against this backdrop (or perhaps within it) was a single vibrating line that did not seem to end, yet was a final end. This was Jacob's worst nightmare, and though he soon became unable to recall it, the fear persisted in the bony crevasses of his subconscious, a deep place where true fear resides. Yukio, a passenger in car number three, and great grandson of a gardener who was killed in the Hiroshima nuclear blast, had the same nightmare as a child, and also could not remember it.

"What are you looking at?" Betty said. The train had become motionless, so she opened her eyes and saw Jacob staring unwaveringly in her direction. Jacob was in a deep reverie and forgot that he was looking at her or the window. He also did not hear her question. "I said, what are you looking at, huh?" Betty's eyes widened at him to get his attention.

"Oh, I'm so sorry, I was just looking out the window and got lost in thought, I didn't mean to stare."

"Uh-huh."

"Really, I'm sorry, I'm too used to looking at people like they're on display, since everyone looks at me that way, being a gaijin—you're American?"

"Yeah, clearly."

"I'm from Seattle, how about you?"

"No you're not."

"Yes, I am, why?" Jacob chuckled nervously.

"Well, I'm from Seattle too, so how about that."

"What part of the city? I'm from Green Lake."

"Ballard for me."

"What brings you to Japan?"

Betty did not tell him. She did not tell him that she was only there to forget. Instead, she invented a few banal responses, spoken with minimal effort and punctuated by periods of silence, until he finally got the picture that she was not interested.

Betty wanted to forget what had led to a recent separation from her husband, and that traveling merely provided her with space and distance, both literal and figurative. It almost did not matter where she traveled to. Closing her eyes to the sun, somewhere foreign where she did not know the language, was the goal. Jacob was intruding this peace. She thought for a moment of reacting with hostility when she caught him staring at her, but then realized that he was just a fly in the ointment, he had no actual ill intent beyond the malignancy of pure happenstance. Five stops later, he changed trains and she never saw him again.

Betty wanted to close her eyes to the sun and retreat into herself, while also being distracted *away* from herself. Betty wished she could return to a time before she was the self she had become, to a self she had ignored for years and years, to a self she was not even sure she knew anymore, and at times a self she doubted she ever was. Regardless, it was the present-self she wanted to forget—she wanted a divorce from this self as much as she wanted a divorce from her husband. Or maybe she did not even want that. She did not truly know.

Betty, or Beatrice as her mother called her, was a young-looking 43 year old woman, petite but with a powerful presence that betrayed her stature. She had red hair though her father was Lebanese (her maiden name was Malouf). Betty would say that it is not all that unusual to be Lebanese and red headed. Her mother was French, or French-Canadian. Many French people have red hair, but that was not as interesting. Her parents raised her without religion. She had been married to a WASP contractor-carpenter named Jim Harris. He had sandy blonde hair that was falling out. He was a good guy, a talented and resourceful guy who built their house from the ground up, on a tear-down lot in Ballard. He was short but masculine. His name sounded masculine, his job was masculine. He drove an olive-green pickup that was sturdy but not showy. He had a strong name that did not confuse anyone, it was simple.

Jim Harris was simple and direct. His life was uncomplicated. He knew what he was good at and he organized his time well. He was the kind of guy who went deer hunting in the fall, skiing in the winter, windsurfing and camping in the summer. Additionally, Betty and Jim would go on several long road trips around the Northwest, to places where they would sample from local breweries and distilleries, though this habit was also well planned. They had two large dogs he bought from special breeders, types of dogs she did not know about before but were clearly masculine choices, one of which Jim took hunting with him. He was soft spoken. He was "handy." He was good at board games and was pleasant at dinner parties.

Jim's family had dinner together on holidays and other special occasions; they would cook together and eat together, calmly and without arguments. This was unlike Betty's folks who did nothing but speak over one another at dinner. And it was her mother who mostly cooked, then guilt tripped them for not helping even though she would start cooking long before anyone got home. Betty's parents also frequently forgot about the holidays, being that they each grew up celebrating different holidays from the American mainstream, holidays her parents no longer engaged with unless around extended family. Betty was an only child. Jim had two younger brothers each with good jobs, both in tech. Jim's family said grace before a meal. Betty's family just ate, she was raised without religion. Her parents would say they were recovering from Catholicism and Islam. Jim's family ate at a table, Betty's family only ate at the table once in a while, with piled-up mail covering most of the surface area. More typically they would eat in front of the T.V., which Betty preferred since there was less arguing—not *no* arguing, just not as much as there was without the T.V. to distract them.

Jim rarely argued, and when he did it was a rather uncomplicated disagreement about something minor. His tranquil yet strong demeanor gave Betty a sense of security she was not accustomed to, although it also gave her a perpetual undercurrent of nervousness. Her father, though not abusive per se, had a short temper, and his anger was always expressed following a period of quietude. Jim was always in a period of quietude, and he chose his words carefully. Sometimes Betty would try and coax an argument out of him, to get it over with, to confront something that was brewing and would blow up later. To confront what made her nervous. However, there never was anything brewing, Jim was just an even keeled sort of guy.

Jim was also very healthy, and his family was healthy. Betty's father was a heavy smoker, which helped him through the hardships of being an immigrant workaholic, juggling three general stores he had developed out of nothing but fought to keep afloat. Eventually, however, he acquired the early stages of emphysema and coughed frequently. He tried quitting, but it was difficult for him. Jim's father was a mechanic and a youth leader at their church. He took kids on outdoor adventures in the summer, even well into his retirement. He also went hunting and skiing with his boys every year. Betty's father had a small motored boat that he used for fishing every once in a while. He never took Betty with him, it was more an excuse to be alone, and when he was older, to sneak a few secret smokes. He also rarely caught anything. A few times, he did not even take the boat on the water, he just sat in his truck near the boat launch, smoking and thinking about his life. To justify this solitude, on these dry-boat outings, he would stop by a grocery store and buy a couple of the sort of fish he was supposedly angling for, then pretend he had caught them. Betty and her mother never suspected it. They hardly noticed he was gone.

Around the time she met Jim, Betty's mother had undergone surgery to remove a lump in her breast. She attributed the lump to decades of exposure to fumes in her nail salon, a business she owned and worked at. She did not smoke but she drank a bit, though often in secret, and usually while cooking dinner before anyone was home to help her. Betty and her father took turns doing the dishes. Jim's mother only had a glass of wine now and then during the holidays, or maybe some eggnog. She made quilts with a church group, and she made everyone's stockings for Christmas, each with a special nod to their individual personalities. These stockings changed every few years. She was primarily a homemaker but she did work as a substitute teacher. She made her sons their choice of pancakes, waffles, French toast, or bacon and eggs each morning. Betty had to take the bus to school on her own, since both her parents started the day so early, and she made her own breakfast, most typically cereal or toast, and never had any bacon (something her father could never bring himself to eat, nor could he stand the smell of it). Betty's mother would most often return home first and have a sacred hour or two to be alone. Jim's mother never thought about being alone, nor yearned for it.

Betty worked as a senior lecturer in the biology department of the University of Washington. She had both a science degree in biology, specializing in the gut flora of sheep, and was a doctor of veterinary medicine, so there was a wide array of subjects she could teach. That made her employable but budgets and politics kept her at the glass ceiling of senior lecturer, never advancing to tenure track. Nevertheless, she was happy with her position. When Betty's mother became sick once more, when they found a tumor on her uterus, she convinced her mom (partly as a joke) to donate her uterus, tumor and all, to a lab in her department. The operation had an uncomfortable potential of mortality, but the joke/promise helped Betty's mother to distract her mind from the fear—it was her kind of humor, Betty knew her mother well. After the procedure, internal bleeding persisted for days, unknown to the surgeon or her mother until it was too late. Betty made it to the ER after she got the call from her father, moments before her mother passed. Betty's mother did not want to be alone.

Jim was on a work site when Betty got the call from her dad. He would have dropped everything and driven his truck to the hospital, but Betty did not want him there. She was not sure why. After some finagling, she was able to get the uterus to her lab. She and other professors would show Pre-Med students the uterus and tumor. She would hold the uterus and tumor, and she would be close to her mother in this way. She felt close to her own self too, to her origin, to a self she once knew, to her old self she wanted to remember, and farther from the new self she wanted to forget. Betty thought that she had cheated her mother's death in a much more poignant and lasting way than a tombstone or urn. And in a way her own death too. Or maybe it would allow this new self to die and leave Betty to be her own authentic self, her better self. But she had to forget. Maybe it was Jim she needed to forget. Jim's family prayed for her mother. Betty was raised without religion.

Time was speeding up for Jim. Time was in fact speeding up for everyone, ever since the Hiroshima nuclear blast ripped a hole in the space-time continuum—not from the explosion itself but from the sudden loss of life, and the sudden desperation. Never before had such widescale human suffering and death happened in less than a second. Jim was merely one of the few to be cognizant of this change in time which, after nearly a century, was beginning to increase exponentially. Jim, a man who was so excellent at organizing his time, perceived the very substance of time to be fading. As time was getting faster, existence was becoming lighter. It was a light decision for Betty to leave, he thought. The houses he had built were becoming lighter, so light they could float up with the dust devils, never mind tornados. He used to consider these homes to be like an anchor that would keep time in place, palpable and present. A mark he had made on time. The houses gave weight to his bones. Now his bones were lighter, not so masculine, fragile, like the hollow bones of a bird. But he could not fly to Japan to find her, he just could not. He was not sure why. Betty was finding herself once more, her better self she had said. Maybe that did not include him anymore.

His first night alone, he had a sad realization: somewhere in there, in the deep knotted muscles of his shoulders, there was a wound. It was not just the knots from years of construction work, the wound went deeper, sunken into an abyss beneath muscle and blood. If only someone could touch that wound, maybe it would break the time spell. If only someone could touch the wound before it turned into necrotic tissue. Maybe then time would go back to normal. Maybe this wound was beyond him, maybe it was interconnected with everyone else, with Betty. He did not really know.

It was discovered that summer of 2025 that a black hole was sucking up everything in the galaxy. Jim imagined that this blackhole was like a giant water bug, and so the blackhole began to take on the shape of a water bug whenever scientists observed the cosmic phenomenon. Others saw a mushroom shape. Or it simply was, as blackholes typically are, a vacuum, empty and dark. One result of the sucking up of space was that time was speeding up. The water bug also sucked up the pain Jim thought he would feel after Betty left, either that or the bug lived within him, where it sucked the pain down below the knots on his shoulders. The pain he felt when Betty left was an initial blow, after that he just had sore shoulders.

The giant water bug (belomastid, toe-biter, alligator tick, what have you) is a curious sort of predator. It will attach itself to a stationary object in a body of water and there await its victim. It will remain completely still (and silent as the grave) until the current of chance brings an unsuspecting prey. It will grab the poor creature with its forelimbs and bite, using its piercing rostrum mandible to inject a potent saliva. This injection of its spit is not only excruciatingly painful but works as a digestive enzyme. That is to say, once the prey has been stunned by its nose-mouth poison, the hideous bug digests the animal from the inside out, sucking on the victim's innards through a small perforation. This digestive process can leave the animal as a mummified shell, which will sometimes deflate like a popped balloon. Jim understood that there was a small perforation in his marriage that he did not know was there before, a hole that leaked-in destructive juices which made their relationship hollow. The painful bite that made this pin prick only Betty noticed at first, but she said nothing. Instead, she forgot who she was, until the day she decided to find herself once more. She had a sabbatical coming up that she had never mentioned to Jim (she initially thought it would be a surprise, but then as the date approached she just kept it to herself). The sabbatical was originally meant for "research," and was considered by her university an "exceptional circumstance" being that she was a non tenure track instructor. For over a year, Betty had saved the funds to cover the semester without ever explaining to Jim what she was doing. By the time Jim realized what was happening, Betty was walking out the door.

It happened one day, over breakfast, at the kitchen table. Jim was telling Betty about how he had to replace the right rear shock on his truck after his latest fishing trip. Betty, who would usually at least feign interest, seemed to just stare blankly and apathetically into space. Jim paused, then peeked behind him to see what she could be glaring at, then looked back at her. Betty's face remained the same. Moreover, she was completely motionless. Jim stood up and walked over to Betty. He waved his hand past her eyes, but there was no response. He put his right hand on the left side of her face and head.

"Betty, what's wrong?"

Just then, Jim heard a loud poof and a bang, like when the tire blew on his last hunting trip. Then there was a loud hiss. Her face began to sag, as did her body, and she started to drape over the chair like a rag doll. At that moment, Jim heard the sound of Betty's boots walking across the hardwood floor of their living room. She was well dressed and had a duffle bag slung over her left shoulder.

"Betty?! What the hell is going on?!"

Betty opened the front door, looked at Jim with the side of her eye, then rushed out. Their screen door on the other side had a spring that needed to be replaced, so they were always careful not to let it slam. This time, the screen door whacked so hard it made the frame resonate like a tam-tam in a Germanic symphony. Betty got into the taxi that was waiting for her and it immediately drove off, the wheels spinning in a cloud of dust down the recently chip-sealed road. In the house, the sound of leaking air persisted. Jim frantically searched for where the leak might be coming from. He took off all of her clothes in the attempt, which was no easy task, as her body seemed to be melting. And then, after much inspection, he ascertained that the leak was in fact coming from her mouth, go figure.

To stop the leak, Jim used one of his favorite fix-it supplies: duct tape. He then realized that there needed to be a way to get air back into her. He taped her lips around an electric pump meant for the inflatable mattress he took car-camping. After about ten minutes of the pump whirring, he got her body back to normal. Then he added a little extra air, just in case, which happened to make her plump in an attractive way. He then sealed her lips together with a special heavy duty adhesive they used in construction. The next day, he heard on the radio that traffic was backed up on the interstate. He did not want to be late for work. He put Betty in the passenger seat and used the commuter HOV lane, arriving just a few minutes past the hour. He kept the windows in his truck cracked and parked in the shade so that the adhesive would not melt in the heat while she waited for him.

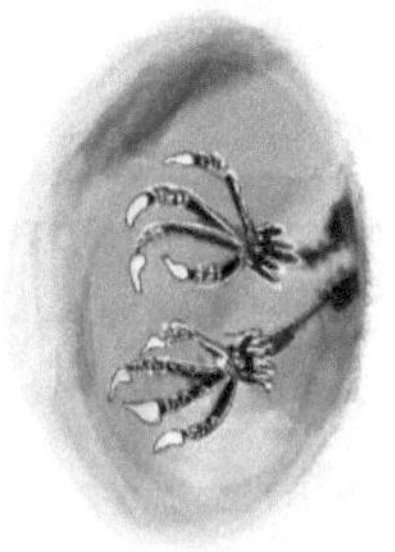

TAMING THE DREW

The crows were restless that day. They exhibited a behavior known officially as "cacophonous aggregation," usually occurring in the presence of a dead conspecific; when one or more crows gather around a fallen comrade and skold (a guttural squawk repeated in short concessions). These calls differ contextually from a simple alarm call to signal danger—the phenomenon is truly a crow funeral (of sorts), though the exact function of the behavior, and whether crows actually possess a

complex understanding of death, is unknown. (How appropriate that a "murder of crows" can also be a funeral).

The crows were restless that day. They skolded and they skolded. They had circled the house since sunrise; an incredible fluttering of wings, a great black mass, a ravenous, murderous funeral of crows. One of their species had hit the kitchen window at the exact right time: the very moment Drew was to answer "what do you have to say for yourself?" He opened his mouth and—bang! The crash took the wind from his voice. His wife Tess thought it was a "sign." Drew was left speechless. He began washing the dishes and propelled himself into muted acts of spring cleaning. The sun rose fully above the horizon. The crows began their skolding, and were as vociferous as they wanted to be.

Then the tranquility of dawn was broken further, beyond repair: not only did the crows continue with their ruckus, but the sun began to glare, garbage trucks clanged, and the neighborhood traffic revved into action. At any minute, their two-year-old daughter, Maddie, would wake. Drew suggested Tess climb into bed, since she blamed him for the all-night argument. Drew had spent most the night giving vague long-winded apologies in response to her vague curt grievances that he did not actually understand (at least, not beyond the simple topic of his negligence in supporting Tess through an issue at work). They could switch parental duties at some point later in the day, Drew said, so he could take a nap too. "Teamwork," he called it.

But the nap for Drew did not come. After Tess woke from her own nap she remained sequestered in their bedroom, confiscating the mattress. Later that evening, once Drew had put Maddie to bed, Tess resumed their argument. It was usual, according to their pattern, for the following argument to transition into warmth and resolve. But times were different.

"I just don't get the support I need from you, I always have to fish for it," said Tess, shaking her head, eyes averted. Then for a second, she made a face as if she was repulsed. "I just can't keep stooping down to your level, I can't engage in these useless discussions with you anymore—I can keep it all to myself."

Tess sat engulfed by a couch-like cushion on the bed, it helped with her back. Tess had injured herself at work and had spent most of the summer in agony. However, she was no longer as restricted to bed rest as she had been. Really, by then she had mostly healed, though a low level of pain persisted, which she clung to.

"What do you mean? I was listening, I support what you say—I really am proud of you for not letting them silence you and speaking your truth, for fighting back... your voice is inspiring," said Drew.

"It feels good to call them out," said Tess. Drew nodded his head in silent approval, eyebrows raised. There was a breath between them that Drew mistook for tenderness.

"Anyway, you're sick of this and not really talking—good night." Tess opened up a book that was in her lap and frowned into the middle of it.

Drew stood in silence, not knowing what to say. Over time he had learned not to trust his words, which always seemed to betray his feelings—he could either say nothing, literally, or say nothing with a long word salad.

"I'm not sick of this," Drew said at length, "I wanted to say that you're not letting them silence you and that's taking back your power. And I'm proud of you for doing that."

Tess shook her head in disapproval. "Your 'listening' is just standing there with that stupid look on your face trying to figure out what I want to hear, and I've had it!" said Tess.

"I love you, I'm sorry baby, I—"

"Don't call me 'baby.' You know, I've had a lot of time in this room to think about how the people who 'love' me have failed me, time and time again, it's extremely depressing."

"I'm sorry Tess, I wish things were different, I just want you to be happy."

"It doesn't make much sense to say, 'I wish things were different'—again, no accountability."

"I'm—"

"No, I don't have time for this nor the emotional reservoir for dealing with how little you are willing to mature and own up to anything."

"Tess, I—"

"I'm over it."

"I'm sorry I've failed you Tess, I really am."

"I don't care if you're sorry, that does nothing for me, the damage is done."

"Please, let me—"

"It's not like I'm asking for a lot, all I want is some love and support, some tenderness, but no—I mean, do you realize how fucked up it was to walk out of the room when I was the sickest I've ever been, just because I made you mad and said means things—when I was drugged out of my mind and in excruciating pain?... I don't know if I can forgive that. You could have killed me by avoiding me and neglecting me in this room."

Drew began trembling with a deep nervousness.

"I'm sorry for the times I walked out of the room in anger, I was weak and responding to my own hurt and stress, I—"

"There you go, flipping the script so that now we're talking about you—I don't think you will ever understand, and I can tell nothing has changed."

"I'm sorry Tess, I'm tired, I didn't nap, my words are coming out differently than I intend, I just want to hold you and—"

"I don't want you to touch me—"

"We could just lay together, and I'll stroke your hair, and—"

"Respect me and listen: I don't want to be touched right now!"

"But you told me before that all you wanted was for someone to hold you and give you love and tenderness—I'm sorry I failed you, I thought I was being supportive, but I see now that I wasn't—let me give you some tenderness, please?"

"Too little, too late."

"Please Tess..."

Their talk carried on like this for some time. Eventually, Tess agreed to lay next to Drew while he ran his fingers through her hair. The sensation was reassuring to Tess, her mother used to gently stroke her hair to help her sleep, or comfort her whenever she was ill. Drew passed his fingers through Tess's hair with a sensual touch, adding little massages of the scalp, and light scratches down her back. Sometimes Drew would work out the tangles in her hair, which Tess did not like much, though she never said anything.

Drew flung himself backwards with a frightened jolt at the sound of Tess's sudden wail. Her horrific screech almost seemed to emanate from another world, echoing throughout their small house with an unnatural reverberation. She jumped from the bed and stood near the wall of the bedroom like a cornered wild animal.

"What's wrong?" said Drew.

Tess shivered in the dark with genuine fear. Drew was afraid too, but he felt that the fear coming from Tess was directed towards him. He was right. Tess moaned and trembled something unintelligible and otherworldly.

"What is wrong?!" said Drew.

"Are you really that evil?" said Tess.

"What did I do?!" said Drew.

Tess noticed the warmth on her shoulder was liquid. She felt her hands.

"Oh my god, I'm bleeding like crazy," said Tess.

Tess ran into the bathroom in the hallway. She turned on the lights and gasped in terror. Drew walked over to her.

"Don't you dare come near me you evil bastard! I'm calling the police, Maddie and I are getting out of here and I'm calling the police, you sick piece of shit," said Tess.

"Tess, please, wha—"

"No don't you—" suddenly Tess could not move or speak, her gaze was fixed on the pleading prayer hands Drew had in front of him. Tess shuddered. Drew looked at his hands as well. Then he fainted.

When Drew came to, he felt a jabbing on his right pectoral region. The back of his head was sore, no doubt from how he had landed on the floor. Maddie was crying from her nursery; the door was open. The jabbing continued until Drew became fully aware— it was Tess nervously poking him with a broom handle. She called to Maddie in as reassuring of a tone as possible, but her voice was still shaky.

"Why are you stabbing me with that?" said Drew.

Tess, seeing that Drew was conscious, took a couple steps backwards and raised the broom handle up like a javelin ready to launch straight at him. Tess's bloodshot eyes glared at Drew with ruby intensity. Drew furrowed his brow in utter bewilderment, and then moved his right hand back to touch the sore spot on his head.

"No, don't!" said Tess, but it was too late.

"Owe! What the goddamn hell is that?!" said Drew.

He looked at his hand: jutting out from the tips of his fingers were razor sharp, curved protrusions. In other words, Drew had grown claws, dripping with the blood from both their scalps. His fingernails had blackened and curled back to make way for the cat-like additions. He felt no pain at the spots of growth; in fact, there was a numbness at his fingertips. This was likely due to the tumescent red orbs that had ballooned under the claws, and which leaked small amounts of an odorless, clear, sappy substance.

Drew tore off his shoes and socks for a desperate look at his feet, giving himself minor cuts in the process. To his relief, Drew's feet had not put out any claws, though the nails were beginning to blacken. The orbs at the toe-ends were there too, but not yet a sickly red color. Rather, they were pink and puffy, reminiscent of the round toes on a baby's feet before flattening after a year or so of walking. The comparison made Drew think of Tess's aunt who, once Maddie was born, annoyingly referred to the phenomenon as "toe berries," and would repeat the saying ad nauseam, as if it could eventually become funny or cute with enough mention.

Drew looked up at Tess.

"What's happening to me?" said Drew. He held up his right hand for support. Tess punched it back with the broom handle.

"Stay where you are," said Tess.

"But, I don't know what's happening to me, please help me," said Drew, and he broke into a heaving sob, as if he were a snoring donkey having bad dreams. The sounds of his weeping funneled, inexplicably, into one long low note, and lingered under Maddie's cries. The whole effect created a morose dial-tone that seemed to make the walls vibrate. Tess began to breathe heavily, ready to explode. She dropped the broom handle, put her hands over her ears, and let out a deafening scream.

The mad cacophony lasted an unreal amount of time, suspending the collective minds of the family in a timeless state of panic. Then, out of the maelstrom, came a loud and persistent knock at the door, and altogether their wailing stopped. Tess snapped away from the hysteria and responded immediately. She rushed into the nursery, grabbed Maddie, then ran past Drew to answer the door. She did not care who it was, only relieved that it was somebody.

Whom she met in the doorway were two male officers. Neighbors had heard the commotion and called the police.

"He's in there," said Tess.

She pointed in Drew's direction without looking at him. She acted on the pure impulse of survival and barged forward into the front yard with Maddie in her arms. The officers crept inside cautiously, ready with their weapons. At an intuitive distance from Drew, the men stopped for a moment and stared silently, paused by fearful befuddlement. Drew faced away from the officers, so from the spot that they stood he seemed like some mysterious roadkill on its last few breaths—a convulsing, sobbing, morbid lump. The animal quality aroused a particular suspicion among the officers.

"We're going to have to get the masks," said one to the other.

They walked out to their vehicle and retrieved masks so intricate in design that the apparatus seemed to transform their faces into squid. One officer stayed behind to question Tess, who had been pacing nervously and trying her best to soothe Maddie. The other officer called for an ambulance. "Looks like we have another one," he said.

Soon the ambulance arrived and took Drew away. He was in hospital care for three days. His vitals were fine, but his condition was continuously monitored. There was special medical interest in his case, and not only because of the bizarre symptoms he was exhibiting. An odd pandemic had suddenly spread across the globe; a disease that seemed to target married couples, causing rapid abnormal growths of hair, nails, teeth, etc., in one or both of the spouses. In other words, there was a plague that turned married people into monsters. However, it was still unknown if increased aggression occurred with infected people, and so there was an air of suspicion surrounding patients. Like an animal with a broken leg, no one wanted these people to lash out and bite. The hospital staff mostly avoided Drew for this reason.

On the third day in the hospital, Tess came to visit. She was assured by the doctor there was nothing to fear. The doctor did not cover her face like a squid, though she still wore a regular N95. In just a matter of a few days, faces were being covered everywhere, regardless of gender or marital status, and many public spaces had shut down. Drew wore a mask too. He was excited and relieved to see the top half of Tess's face above the covering. He looked into her deep sapphire eyes and began telling her everything he had experienced since the ambulance came for him. As he spoke, Tess was engaged for a minute (maybe less) but then looked off into that distant place she went to when she waited for him to say something else—words she expected from Drew yet never expected she would hear.

"What's wrong?" said Drew.

"The fact that you even have to ask is pathetic and makes me sad," said Tess.

"I'm sorry, I'm just so excited to see you, I've been going through hell here and I was so worried I'd never see you and Maddie again... I-I'm just anxious to tell you everything... it's been hell."

"And how do think it's been for me? You always just talk about yourself—you talk *at* me, not *with* me—you haven't even asked about my head Drew, I guess you just don't give a shit."

"I'm so sorry Tess, I haven't been in my right mind—of course I care, I love you, how's your head?"

"You don't get to say the words 'I love you' if you hold zero accountability for anything. You did this to me Drew:" Tess leaned forward and showed him the back of her head. Parting back her hair, she displayed an ugly neglected slash that should have had stitches, though thankfully had begun to close.

"Oh my god, I'm so sorry baby, I still can't believe what has happened," said Drew.

"Don't call me 'baby'—to top it off, Maddie has been acting really rowdy lately and jumped on my arm, which has set my progress back a good six weeks, I'm in excruciating pain."

"I'm so sorry you're in pain, I wish I could take it away."

"I can't seem to catch a break. I guess the only thing the physical pain is good for is distracting from the emotional pain."

"I wish you didn't have *any* pain."

"Wishing doesn't cut it, wishing does nothing for me—you know, you've really put us through hell, and as usual there's no accountability on your end, I have to do all the work. You only have to 'wish' and do nothing else."

"Tess—" Drew reached into his usual bag of words but found it was empty. Tess had an empty bag too. Silence filled a space that was vacant between them. Their exhausted bags lay limp and lifeless on the sterile hospital floor, inventing nothing.

Tess was anxious to return to Maddie, who was being watched by a friend, so they took the silence with them into mandated quarantine. And oh, but of course, it was no easy task releasing Drew from the hospital. The bureaucratic delay, on point of his pandemic-caused affliction, was inhumanely sluggish. It took all day. Nevertheless, the resulting dull headache of clerical process (so familiar to stuffy zones of grey carpet, white walls, and jars of pens) helped to numb the aching undercurrent that flowed quietly beneath them.

Once at home, they likewise sank into an abyss of numb routine, directed by the laconic whisper of muscle memory. For a week, maybe more, Drew fell back into the motions of cooking meals, taking care of Maddie, doing chores, and serving Tess as she recouped from her injury in bed. At night, after Drew had given Maddie a bath and sang her to sleep, Tess most often moved to the living room. Though Tess and Drew would speak words to one another, the deeper silence was still there, nullifying the meaning of utterance, shrouding intimacy. What they discussed at night was a scripted binary of either forced-giddy banalities or a detached review of what was wrong with the world. However, there soon came an evening where Tess decided to recognize, for a moment, that sad undercurrent which had, in the meantime, swollen into a flood.

As part of their usual banter, Drew had made an innocuous joke, to which he laughed far more than he really cared to. Tess glared into his vacuous eyes. She saw in him the pathetic indulgence of routine as a substitute for truth—he had accepted the routine, he had accepted the numbness, he had accepted his very condition, and all for the sake of looking away from that flood that was swirling around them. She saw a coward, and it infuriated her. She saw a monster wearing rubber gloves so he could not cut anything, yet neither could he *touch* anything. He did not touch her. She asked herself if he had ever *truly* touched her. She did not want him to touch her. And she saw too his desperate grasps for any shreds of happiness, for shallow echoes of glee, for tiny bits of joy; salivating over scraps that fell from the table of their old life, like a dog. She pitied him for that. Her pity muffled her anger, and she was silent. She dropped onto the scraps-covered floor with him, stuffing her mouth with pity, and her stomach with the resentment that followed.

Drew's symptoms continued to progress. The claws appeared on his toes. The hair on his limbs became thick and shaggy. His canines descended and showed over his lower lip, even when his mouth was closed. Drew's dental growth inflamed his gums. Sometimes, his gums issued out an orangish liquid, like a leaky faucet filled with rust. The first time his gums bled like this, it triggered his eyes to water. Since the hospital, he had held back tears over his change. But at this moment, his body commanded the tears.

He wept in the bathroom, secretly. He could not help but look in the mirror as he did this, seeing the effusion of blood and tears pour ghoulishly from his face, while catching the fluids in the sink.

Drew's hearing had become heightened, or that is what he thought. It was far more likely that his mounting anxiety (which he perpetually denied) caused him to be skittish at the slightest sound. The noises that disturbed him most were mechanical. Hence, he began to view the house as a shelter from the mechanical world outside. The park by their home was the only place he went to. The park was a shelter too—down by the banks of a fast-flowing river, Drew was unable to hear most of the hiss from a nearby highway. He would play with Maddie on the many thin beaches and groves along this river. Maddie liked to collect the wild rose hips that grew in the riparian woodland. "Beautiful colors," she would say. Maddie liked the white snowberries as well. Under the leaves of a patch of tansies they would look for fairies. And her papa would skip rocks for her where the water was relatively calm. (The crescent shape of his claws gave a special spin to the flat stones that made them bounce across the water an amazing number of times). Maddie would always laugh when Drew skipped rocks, it was magic to her. They had a little world in the park that became like a sanctuary from the ubiquitous motor, though he could still faintly hear its odious scream off the highway, ever near.

When life events fell off center for Drew, he would force his perspective back into the narrow focus he felt safe in, such as the little world of a park that shielded him from traffic. Or gloves that covered claws. It was an unnatural squeeze of perspective, like a horse wearing blinders. Drew's actual center was mysterious and secretive. He did not want others to know what was at the bottom of him. He thought that if people knew, he would be left alone.

Deep roots scared Tess.

Their small home had a large garden space around it. When they first rented the house, before Maddie was born, Drew developed big plans for the garden. He put in a tremendous amount of sweat and labor into clearing bushes, working the soil, pruning trees. He constructed a hedge with an archway out of young aspen, flower beds, and vegetable patches. He pruned trees with a naturalistic aesthetic, and he got a coop together with several chickens. He was by no means a professional gardener, but Drew was devoted (as best he could in his spare time) to learning about gardening. Thus, gardening became a topic that frequently occupied his mind—he wanted to understand more than the mere mechanics of gardening, he wanted to know what it meant, or what it meant to him. Tess, on the other hand, was not a big part of this garden planning, which she resented. Indeed, Drew had not actively included Tess; gardening became for Drew a medium by which he could apply his center, so he was not thinking about much else. Yet neither did he exclude her.

The few times that Tess did openly express an interest in helping with the garden, such as weeding and turning soil, she felt a cryptic pain in the action of uprooting plants and digging into the earth. She felt like she was violating something. The roots of unwanted plants, exposed and tossed nonchalantly onto a pile, seemed perverse to her. There was a nostalgia there as well, but she would not quite call it that. She did not know what to call it. But maybe it was an echo from her past that slept under a gossamer quilt of the subconscious—palpable but not known.

Tess was afraid of deep roots.

As a child, her family moved from place to place. She soon learned that roots which were shallow hurt less when pulled from the ground.

Maddie did not know about roots, not yet.

Drew stood by the kitchen sink, washing dishes. The tips of his claws were nifty points that could scrape the crud hiding in crevices. Then Tess emerged, unexpectedly, from the bedroom. Maddie noticed her mama at once. The light that filtered through a thin curtain caressed the pallor of Tess's face, making her glow like a midday moon. She smiled at Maddie with real, inexhaustible joy, a primordial joy that could not be worn away, no matter how ill she felt. She kept this joy only for Maddie, it was deep and sacred.

Tess embraced Maddie with fragile strength—a preternatural strength that overwhelmed the weakness in her body. Tess held on to this sensation dearly. And, smiling, she looked up to Drew, seeking in his eyes a tender reflective amplitude, like a lighthouse. Instead, Tess noticed the pathetic facade of a forced smirk. Like a spent match, the light went out, and she hated herself for allowing Drew such profound influence on her. The smoke and sulfur of the spent match watered her eyes and her lips quivered. She took a breath to speak but her voice cracked at the first syllable. She closed her eyes a moment and tried again.

"You know Drew, you really have some sick control issues," said Tess.

Drew's face tingled. A mild shock ran through his body. The shock was mild because he predicted darts to be thrown by Tess unpredictably; though his face still tingled because they were *not* predictable, and it stung. He spoke through his teeth, holding back some anguish.

"What are you talking about?" said Drew, walking over to Tess.

"Look around you Drew, do you see any evidence of me?" Drew knew what she was suggesting, so he did not look. "You can't come up with anything, can you? Not really. I have no control over decorating this house, the kitchen, the garden, the car, what and when I eat—I have to depend on you for everything, even for a goddamn glass of water while I'm stuck in that goddamn room, in pain, and I hate it."

"But that's not me trying to control anything, Tess, I—"

Tess scoffed and cut Drew short. "I can't believe that's your response, wow. You know what, I'm done. If that's how you're going to respond, then I am done!"

"Done with what Tess?" Drew knew this was a stupid question, but he wanted her to just say it fully.

"Do I have to spell it out for you? I don't even have a say in how we raise our child—"

"That's because I have to take care of everything!" said Drew. He glared intensely, then threw his paws up and scuttled back to the kitchen sink, aggressively turning the faucet to its maximum water volume.

"There you go, running away again whenever we have an argument—you get to do whatever want you want, when you want. Meanwhile, I am stuck in that room alone and can't even go to the bathroom when I need to because Maddie will see me in the hallway and get upset." Tears began to penetrate through Tess's voice, though her anger was undiminished.

Drew stared straight into the sink. Gray suds sloshed down the dingy dark drain. He attempted to be stoic. "I have to take care of everything, I don't just do what I want."

"So, you're not going to acknowledge that you leave me alone in a room all day and night without any control over whether I live or die?"

"I have to raise our child."

"You think I want any of this?"

Drew stood silent, washing dishes.

"Drew, I'm not going to talk to you like this, either you respect me and talk to me over here like an equal or it's over."

"I'm too upset, I need to do dishes."

"Fine, then it's over—Maddie, we're leaving."

In what seemed like an instant to Drew, Tess had Maddie in one arm, keys and a purse in the other, and was walking to the front door.

"No, wait!" Drew ran towards them and grabbed Tess's hand.

"Let go of me!"

Tess jerked her hand away with the muscular force of her whole body, yet the tip of Drew's index claw had poked through the dish glove and so slashed her palm. She crouched, letting Maddie down, and began to shiver. She released breathy exclamations of pain, her body subtly writhing from both the shock of her injury and her emotional state. Some blood dripped on the floor.

"Oh Tess, I'm so sorry darling—please, apply pressure, I will get some bandages and alcohol."

"I don't want you to take care of me, you've shown me how dangerous that can be."

"Tess, you need help."

"I don't want *your* help."

Maddie came over and hugged Tess's back, applying pressure to her bum shoulder. Tess smiled through a wince and was about to tell Maddie she loved her, but Drew interrupted. He noticed the discomfort Maddie caused and gently ushered some space between her and her mama. Drew thought he was being conscientious, though instead removed the only true source of comfort Tess had left. She wondered if Drew was the great interrupter in her life, if he was in fact malicious toward her, a persistent cloak and dagger. She sneered and widened her eyes up at him, as if she now knew the secret truth behind it all.

"You're evil! You're vile!" said Tess.

In about the space of an hour, and with what was clearly uncontrollable bleeding, Drew was able to convince Tess to let him drive her to the hospital.

Tess's accusations of insidious malevolence Drew was unable to process, he could not hear them. Such notions drifted, like flotsam and jetsam, on the great tide of his denial—Drew could not face the deterioration of their marriage, and so he became vehemently ordinary, abrasively usual, stunningly normal. He interacted with Tess like a postcard. He gave her all that was to be expected of "family." Tess knew he was buying time, but she was too tired to resist. She needed a few days to rest her hand, which now had several stitches—Tess allowed Drew the charade and made her own plans. She called her mother.

When Tess's mother flew in, a day or so later, it was made clear to Drew that she was leaving with Maddie and going back home to her parents' place. She emphasized the word "home."

Tess had suggested to Drew that he and Maddie go to the pool, or on a hike. Drew should find something "fun to do" on their "last day," she said. Drew did not wish to do anything out of the ordinary. His lack of enthusiasm to "do something special" was falsely interpreted by Tess and her mother as a sign of callousness. Drew could not communicate to them the significance of a regular day. True, the thought of a grand outing exhausted him, but it was an exhaustion produced by putting to the side what his heart held dear. Drew could not explain to Tess and her mother that it was the daily routine of his life with Maddie that he knew he would miss the most, because he would no longer have it. He thought that he may, perhaps one day, have an opportunity to hike with Maddie, to experience a special occasion with her, but no longer would he be able to live out a normal day. No longer would Drew be an ordinary presence in Maddie's existence, nor would he be part of her daily rhythms. Drew would never again be associated with the passing of time: the phases of the moon, the seasons, the tide, and all the steps between mileposts. Drew just wanted one last ordinary day.

Drew went through his routine with Maddie as if he were already experiencing a distant memory, attempting to suspend time by soaking in each and every detail. At the park, Maddie wanted to play in the field. A row of wild tansies attracted her curiosity, as it usually did. Maddie would inspect their little yellow flowers— "buttons for the fairies," they would say. Maddie would run and play around a lush willow tree on the edge of the field. Drew would make "laurel" crowns out of the young willow branches and place them atop Maddie's head of golden curls. She would run out into the field, proudly skipping to some great victory. Drew would yell "she lifts cheering crowds onto their feet—yay Maddie!" She would run back and say "lay on the grass." Then they would fall back together onto the lawn and face the clouds. "The big sky!" Maddie would exclaim. This day was no different.

Except, however, for a slender plume of smoke Drew noticed on the horizon, rising like an apparition above a nearby hill. It was then that Drew was taken from the spell of their play, for a pause. He became cognizant of the fact that Maddie's memory will not retain these moments; moments that will at best become an impression. By contrast, Drew became keenly aware of how the minutiae of their routine would be etched into his mind forever. Moreover, that this moment which was so predictable, so usual, so precious, would never be enacted again. The sky that was so blue, softly bedecked with clouds of imagined animals, seemed locked in time, yet at its end.

After they flew thousands of miles away with Tess's mother, the smoke filled the valley for weeks. The forest on the hills turned black, the garden flowers choked and writhed into crippled pathetic lumps.

Smoke and mirrors—during this smokey time, Drew kept in contact with Maddie through that sad mirror called a "phone." Drew would speak to Maddie as best he could to a mirror, sent to another mirror, held close to the face of a fidgeting toddler. She seemed distant beyond the distance. Drew could tell that the little world they had together was fading. He told himself that deep within she would never forget. Life was fun where she was, a point that was made clear to him by Tess and her parents—they spent a lot of money on Maddie's toys and experiences, and so she had what Drew could never give her. The world he had had with Maddie meant nothing to them, it had no real value; Maddie knew what was valuable now.

Over time, Tess refused all contact with Drew. To speak with Maddie, he had to go through Tess's parents. Contact from Drew was not helping Tess heal. Their interactions retraumatized her and reopened the wounds that Drew had left behind. Granted, the physical wounds had long since repaired, but under the scar tissue festered something metaphysical. Tess had told Drew that the "first cut was the deepest," but that the slash to her scalp was not actually the first. The first cut was when he had "left her in a room to die." Tess asserted that she could have died in that room, neglected by Drew. He just did things as he wanted, when he wanted, and did not care for her or put her first, she said.

Drew's memory was different. But he had claws, he could not trust himself.

One desperate night, Drew called Tess using the speakerphone feature of his new landline (his claws had become too long and cumbersome to operate the touchscreen of a mobile phone, or to even properly hold the landline handset). He called and called, until finally she answered. She explained to him that the virus was just a manifestation of how he treated her, his "true colors." The fact that he must have concealed his *real* self from her for years is what disturbed her most.

"How am I supposed to continue in this relationship when you hid who you were all this time?" said Tess.

Drew reflected. He pictured his inner beast to the point where it took on genuine shape. The thing was somehow familiar to him. He saw it as having persisted through his life, always there. A shameful aspect of himself. A deluge of guilt came over him.

"It wasn't right of me, I'm sorry. It was toxic to hide that part of myself, but it comes from shame. It is difficult to expose myself like that to others, I'm sorry," said Drew.

"I can imagine, but a healthy loving relationship involves people being completely honest with each other... and I never felt that with you... and now I know why."

"I'm sorry Tess."

"I always thought I had to change how I really felt for you to what you expected from me because you 'know' me."

"What? That doesn't make—"

"Don't interrupt. I'm not the Tess you 'love.' I'm not as simple as someone's wife. I don't think that's right for me... You didn't let me be myself... This can't continue—I need to be free. I need to feel liberated. I just want to love myself and go back to who I really am, not the person you convinced me I was."

"I didn't let you be yourself?"

"When I tell my old friends the bullshit you convinced me of, they are shocked—so shocked that I let you make me think I was a self-absorbed, manic depressive, manipulative person. I am not that at all."

"I said that to you?"

"In so many words. You were so cruel, and you controlled me... Well, you can't anymore and I want my freedom."

"I'm sorry if I ever convinced you of such terrible things. I don't want to control you." Drew's head felt like a cannon ball. His hands like the salty unfathomable ends of a lobster. His toes like worms. His body like straw stuffed in rags. Drew was itchy from the straw, and it nauseated him. He trembled.

"'If'?! Drew, you did."

"Listen, I'm in a lot of pain right now, I don't know how much longer I can do this, but I do think it's important to talk… I'm just hurting right now."

"I am hurting too, and I'm sorry this is difficult for you, but you need to respect me. I told you I need my space and so far you have not granted me that."

"I didn't mean to disrespect you. I'm sorry."

"You continue to constantly."

"I'm just in pain."

"You're being selfish. I am in so much pain your pain does not compare, and yet again here I am talking to you and trying to do what you want, when you want… oof, I'm furious now, furious that I'm even talking to you because you are not respecting my boundaries."

"My pain is not unimportant."

"OK, I'm done. That's your response? It tells me everything I need to know. Goodnight. Please don't contact me again."

"Wait! I don't want to disrespect your boundaries, I didn't mean to do so tonight. I'm sorry Tess, I know I've hurt you—please, let's talk again soon."

"I just tried with you and you've broken my trust, again. I can't keep making myself vulnerable despite having very little strength left, and still needing to heal. I have begged, fucking begged you, Drew, to put yourself in my shoes, and you don't… I'm done."

"Tess?" The air was dead. Drew leaned into this silence, as if he could communicate something via her waning presence. Then, with the fumble of a claw, there was a dial tone. He was incredulous to her absence, it felt unnatural. His emotions felt unnatural. He had no grasp of center, nor could he navigate via any self-identifying markers—such signage had all been blown down by the cold obliterating winds of a dial tone. He was exposed now to the elements. He was an animal on some desolate plain, dumbfounded and alone, stripped of culture, imbued with a searing and somber brutality.

Drew would read to his daughter as he gave her a bath. Maddie's favorite story was about a wild girl who befriends a bear. High up in the mountains, the wild girl was far removed from all other humans; she knew only the animals and the sheer, insurmountable peaks that stretched out into infinity. Sometimes, the wild girl would cry out from a high point and then listen for a human reply—she heard none, only her echo. Drew would ask Maddie what an echo was. Maddie would emphatically say "the sound bounces off it—boom!—and comes back to your ear." Maddie demonstrated the ricochet of sound by moving her hand back and forth between her and the bathtub wall. Drew was proud of such complex understanding at Maddie's young age.

But Drew was beginning to discover that there are other kinds of echoes. Drew heard Maddie's echo-explanation now, though she was not there. He heard, faintly, their routine interactions that were sacred to him. The bathtub was empty, yet it was filled with an ethereal supply of bubbles, toys, laughter—cries not to get into the bath, cries not to get out of the bath. The tile walls of the shower above the tub were still covered by the faded crayon murals they had created: animals and characters born of a special space that exists only between parent and child. This space was gone from the house, as if the heart of its structure had been exposed by some existential vivisection, and then removed. Drew felt as if the house was abandoned, as if he were a lost soul in the desert and only sought its confines for shelter—to sleep in a tomb which preserved the memory of another world. Drew had not changed anything, he only let dust and the movement of time modify any part of this tomb.

Drew wandered alone in the park. He heard the echo there too: carrying Maddie on his shoulders through a field of tiny white flowers, looking at bees and butterflies. The shapes of the little flowers, appearing on thick, soft, lush shrubs, had evaded them. One could draw a rose or a tulip or even an orchid from memory, but these miniscule flowers held to an amorphous petal that glimmered in the summer sun and seemed to slow time. Drew floated in that field now, hovering above it, though the flowers had already shriveled and passed. He walked up a small incline to a raised path. The rocks he kicked up while walking rolled down the slope and knocked into one another, unseen. The sounds clashed somewhere out of Drew's consciousness, beyond human knowing, left only to the beetles and lizards, the primal energy that welled up around Drew as if he were the last human on Earth. Then he remembered he was a beast.

Drew walked on, beyond the fields, down a trail that led to the woods. The walkway went by a small tributary, then slipped under an overpass to get to the riparian groves along the banks of the main river. A beaver had made a dam on the stream near the path, which created a small pond. A lodge was built under an old willow tree, partially submerged by the beaver's pond. The cars roared above Drew as he paused to look at the lodge. The water vibrated with life. Drew waited for a large truck to pass over and then shouted a loving, simple exchange he often had with his daughter—the traffic noise concealed the words of the phrase. The dark waters of the pond resonated with the primal energy that engulfed him, and would doubtless one day swallow up all of humanity.

Drew walked on through to the woods. He stood by the roaring flow of the river. The leaves in the forest were beginning to lose chlorophyll and so were "changing color." Really, the leaves were fading. But their decay was beautiful, and their death of mulch on the forest floor smelled sweet and gave a gentle cushion for Drew's paws as he stepped. The leaves were mostly cottonwood and aspen. The leaves were heart shaped—Drew had never noticed before. Drew took one leaf and let it fall gently onto the river. It was a message of his love, and it was a question of his love. A gust of wind hit the branches above, and a torrent of orange leaves showered upon him. He had his answer—or perhaps it was wishful thinking. Perhaps it was only the wind, perhaps it was only the rhythm of the seasons, the annual decay of things. Perhaps his answer was decay. He did not know. He only knew that he wanted love too.

Drew closed his eyes. Behind his lids there was a deeper forest, one that stretched out into infinity. Out of this mystical landscape appeared a monster. She crept through the dark undergrowth like a tiger. Her eyes were emerald, her hair cascaded over her body in thick waves; it was impossible to know where her body was. Her hands and feet had severe claws. Her canines were long and sharp, continually lacerating her luxurious lower lip, the blood from which was her rouge. She approached him gently. They could not embrace, because they would cut each other in the process—claws had begun to extend, generously, from their ribs. They likewise could not kiss, nor could they hold hands. She pushed her nose forward and Drew touched the end of his nose to hers. His nose was wet and cold and had developed an extreme sensitivity to touch—it was not an act they could sustain. They broke away from contact. Drew then offered the back of his wrist. Their wrists touched. Then she put forward her kneecap and their knees touched. Then the tops of their heads, their elbows, their ears, their shoulders.

Then there was nothing, he touched nothing. No sound, no breeze, no insects, no falling leaves, only a timeless moment of emptiness. He could suffocate in this stillness. His lungs had no breath. Perhaps this was a moment between heart beats… Drew then found his breath, the rush of flowing water flooded his ears, birds sang, a gentle gust touched his brow. His pulse returned. But his heart sank.

Drew wandered aimlessly. As dusk was gathering, he came to the park boundary. Beyond was an area of farmland at the base of some rugged hills. He had never walked there before, and truly, he had no desire to then. But he continued in that direction, drawn by a listless current of apathy. Then it was dark. Drew noticed an empty stable filled with bales of straw. He laid down on a flat section and so made a bed for the night. This meager shelter seemed almost luxurious to him. The straw, however, began to slip under his clothing and itch, so he disrobed—first by daintily attempting with his claws to unfasten buttons and zippers, but then resorting to carelessly tearing his garments off... His slumber was deep and dreamless.

In the morning, Drew awoke to shrieks, and then the slamming of the stable gate. It was locked and reached up to the roof; there was no outlet. With a burst of energy, he shook the bars wildly like a chimp in the circus. But it was brief. Also like so many circus or zoo animals, he found a dark corner, sat with his back to any potential audience, and fell silent.

TELEMARKETER

The crows were restless that day. They exhibited a behavior known officially as "cacophonous aggregation," usually occurring in the presence of a dead conspecific; when one or more crows gather around a fallen comrade and skold (a guttural squawk repeated in short concessions). These calls differ contextually from a simple alarm call to signal danger—the phenomenon is truly a crow funeral (of sorts), though the exact function of the behavior, and whether crows actually possess a complex understanding of death, is unknown. (How appropriate that a "murder of crows" can also be a funeral).

The crows were restless that day. They skolded and they skolded. They had circled the house since noon; an incredible fluttering of wings, a great black mass, a ravenous, murderous, funeral of crows. One of their species had inhaled an excess of silica dust, kicked up by cars all summer long after the residential streets were chip-sealed. Ted knew "crow language." That is, he had come up with a system for psychically interpreting crow vocalizations (it was mostly an intuitive process). He listened to their skolds in hopes of making sense of it.

Ted had been displaced by wildfires scorching the west—a recent fire had burnt his entire neighborhood to a blackened crisp, up in the mountains above Monterey Bay. In addition, Ted had lost his job after a global pandemic shut down the hostel he worked for. Now elderly, and having devoted the majority of his life to playing music while surviving on "day jobs," Ted had hardly any money or security beyond his meagre social security check. After the fire hit, he had little choice but to move in with Mark, his stepson.

A long while back, Ted and Mark's mother (who was then newly divorced) had met, both being musicians in a small town—he played guitar and Mark's mother the piano. Mark learned to channel his own creative energy into his studies. Eventually, he became an adjunct English professor for a small university, up north. There were wildfires there too. Mark and Ted breathed a thick smoke the day the skolds came, with the large murder flapping over one dead crow. The skolds were too frenetic in nature to employ Ted's method of interpretation but he knew there was something off. The smoke was bad. Ted and Mark prayed for bad weather.

The actual flames of the wildfires had not reached the valley where Mark lived. There had been, however, one evening when Mark stepped outside to watch the fires dance down the side of a hill just three miles from his home, though firefighters prevented it from moving across the valley floor. The fires stayed, almost magically, in the hills and mountains—vast and incomprehensible. The destruction to life was hardly noticed by most people, let alone even thought of—countless creatures felt the flesh tear from their bones whilst tree giants could not utter one syllable of oxygen to console them, choking centuries of life away— like ancient sages being silenced forever. And in a momentary blaze, unseen and uncared for, the sages were then forgotten.

The smoke from their funeral pyre penetrated the lives of those in the valley, and across the west the story was similar. Yet, not only were the people befuddled by the devastation that originated their poisonous air, but there was also a pandemic, a plague which ravaged and bit them through the smoke. Mass graves were dug. What little care people held for life outside their screens and windows billowed into oblivion as serenely as the dark plumes from the forest, dimming the sky. No one went out to see it. No one went out much at all, they were all petrified of the plague. Their lungs were as numb as their hearts—the plague was already infecting through the air, so why then would the smoke matter? People did not expect the air to be clean anymore.

Ted had moved in just a few days after Mark's wife had moved out, taking their daughter with her. Mark had not seen Ted for many years but they had remained close by way of frequent telephone conversations. After Ted and Mark's mother had divorced, Ted did not actually *need* to stay in touch with Mark, who was still a child at the time. He did not have to visit with Mark on several occasions, nor did he have to speak to him on the phone regularly over the years, offering advice, or just to chat. But Ted cared for Mark and recognized that he was the closest to a son that he ever was likely to have. Ted never said that out loud, and probably did not even think it loudly to himself, but it was nonetheless an accepted truth secretly understood between them. When Ted told Mark about his predicament, Mark said that he could stay as long as he wanted. Ted took that literally.

Ted had moved several times since his divorce from Mark's mother. One of the places he rented, a cabin in the redwoods, had a faulty heater that leaked carbon monoxide. It was not enough to kill him, but it poisoned him chronically for months. He became extremely ill before he realized what the issue was, and it took years to recover (though he never did fully regain his health and vitality). In those first months, he lost work, maxed out credit cards, and swept through his puny savings. His landlady, fearing a lawsuit, let him stay in the cabin for a while, but within a year she realized how limited his legal powers truly were and kicked him out. He was meant to feel fortunate that he was not formally evicted.

Luckily, in the last few months of cabin-living, Ted had recovered just barely enough strength to finagle a little under-the-table work. And so, he was able to squirrel away a small but easily exhaustible monetary reserve. He also had a van that he could sleep in. He put his belongings in storage and drove down the coast, aimless, moving from campground to campground. The smoke from the campfires hurt his lungs. He lived off of canned fish, rice cakes, and lettuce. He pawned some guitars and what little else of value he had stuffed into his van so that he could extend his fruitless venture toward an inevitable bad ending, and to keep the hope of his storage unit alive. Mark spoke with him over the phone during these times, when Ted could afford it. Mark told Ted he could live with him then, but Ted was embarrassed. These were not "normal" problems to have. And thus, through societal shame, he held onto some residue of the middle class, skimmed from its thin veneer, and slept in his van.

Finally, there came the time when all resources were completely gone. He did not know how he was going to eat the next day, or how he would pay for gas. He was running on empty both figuratively and literally. He wandered around the little foggy coastal town he had come to, ghostlike, unseen by anyone, stripped of his humanity.

Nevertheless, Ted wanted to be around people. Yet without any money whatsoever, and it being so cold in the fog, his only real and free option was the communal area of a youth hostel (provided they failed to notice he was not a guest). He hoped that he could sit, be warm, and be in the presence of others, even if he himself was not part of the social interaction. He had the vague idea that he could at least observe the connections between others (at this time, people still spoke to one another in public scenarios and even made eye contact). Ted sat for a few hours, listened to the general murmur of people in conversation, and watched the afternoon light wane into early evening. The growing dark caused his hunger-heavy eyes to close and he drifted into sleep. When he awoke an hour or so later, he noticed a "help wanted sign" by check-in. He applied the next day and started work, checking in guests, changing sheets, doing laundry, etc.

It took a while to move out of his van (and sometimes the hostel) and into a rented place of his own. And it took a while to make a few genuine friendships, but he had some small purpose in this job. He eventually bought back the favorite of his guitars, and he even used the hostel's communal area to perform on occasion. In this way, music crept slowly back into his life, which gave him added purpose. And all the while, he sustained the storage unit up north—in it was the promise of a life he could unpack and return to one day. He kept this hope alive. And among the possessions were the remaining artifacts of his marriage to Mark's mother, from their brief time together as a family. In part, he kept that hope alive too, the hope of resurrecting a dead past from the ashes of sentiment.

There were also many things in storage that had no value whatsoever, such as bags of random papers, knickknacks, and so on—the contents of what Ted's mother used to call "hell drawers," along with the piles and stacks of junk that Ted's mother would have draped a cloth over and proclaimed "phew, that covers a multitude of sins." The worthless material filled the gaps of empty space within the unit, making the storage full and complete. The trash made his past full and complete, so that he did not have to face the vacuous vagaries that perplexed his personal history. The years he bandaged with an indifference to isolation, or the years he wounded with isolation in the name of a broken promise for intimacy, for a "family" that never grew into itself.

Many storage bills later (rarely paid for on time, and with many hustles to keep it afloat), Ted was faced with the circumstances that led him north to Mark's house. He sat deliberating whether he should travel north or stay and sleep in his tiny van by the foggy bay. And then a crow landed on a tree branch above, letting out a calm, slow, deep and resonant caw. According to Ted's system of crow-language, this meant "yes, move north, move in with Mark." Ted left that weekend.

On the way, he stopped at the storage unit with the intention of packing it all into a moving truck, and had everything at the ready to do so. However, once he rolled up the garage-style door and looked directly at the archaeology of his past (for the first time in fifteen years), Ted was hit with an invisible force that stunned him into inaction. He would later say it was because of all the toxic rat shit (which was no doubt present in the low rent unit), and that the pinched nerve in his back prevented him from lifting the bulk of what was there, but something much heavier weighed him down. He did not understand it, so he grabbed a few boxes near the front, free of rat shit, and closed the door. Somehow the rent he paid was worth not having to look at it, yet still preserve it. He drove another 700 miles to Mark's house, with a moving truck that was more than half empty, towing his little cube-shaped car behind him. The photos and home videos he planned to look over with Mark would have to wait until his back healed and he could return to the unit, or so he told himself.

A couple of years later, the storage facility changed ownership. The old owners, in an attempt to cash in as much as possible, cleared out several units, both auctioning the contents (without the consent of the renters) *and* filing an insurance claim. One of their victims was Ted. His mental wherewithal was limited, stifled by paranoia and inertia, so he missed the window to make a police report. In addition, he missed the deadline of speaking with the adjustor. Ted told himself that, in truth, he just wanted it gone, to be free of his past. The reality, however, was that only *part* of him wanted it gone, while the other part of him mourned the loss deeply. To fight over the unit meant to face this loss, and thereby unravel the painful profundity of this loss: not only had he spent thousands over nearly twenty years to keep the unit (which in an instant was gone), but there was no longer much physical evidence to verify his past, or the man that he once was. The unit was all-of-a-sudden empty, like a blackhole that sucked away his very essence, his existential substance. Ted combed through the few belongings he had brought to Mark's house and found only a dozen photos. He showed these to Mark: "72 years and just 12 photos," he said. Mark knew not to pressure Ted into calling the adjustor.

The night Mark learned that Ted's storage had been broken into, and that nothing was left, he had a nightmare. For the first time since early childhood (or was it for the first time?), he dreamt about the "get-you monster." His mother had told him growing up that if he wandered too far the "get-yous" would get him. It was never explained what, exactly, the get-you was though somehow, as an amorphous being, it made sense to Mark. One day, however, the get-you became manifest: Ted put on the wall a Balinese painting that had, peeking from the shadows behind some trees, near a waterfall, an apelike-wolflike monster. Naturally, Mark called it the "get-you painting."

In Mark's dream as an adult, the get-you did not make an immediate appearance. Rather, Mark first had the challenge to face down a large male gorilla. The ape emerged, knuckle-walking, out from behind some bushes, maybe ten or so yards away, and then turned his gargantuan head to look at Mark. He became visibly and audibly agitated. He stood on his hind quarters and walked toward Mark, who was petrified with fear. He beat his chest and bared his teeth. Mark remembered that he had read not to respond to the gorilla, that the gorilla most typically bluffs. Terrified, Mark stood his ground. The gorilla was taken aback somewhat, but the effect of this tactic quickly wore-off. Lifting his huge awe-inspiring arms, the gorilla got ready to crush Mark. In an instant, Mark decided his only recourse was to tickle the great beast. He lunged for the ape's armpits and tickled furiously. Miraculously, this strategy worked; the gorilla clutched his pits, grimaced, and then ran away, hobbling along on his small bowed legs like an old cowboy. But then, Mark had a second challenge. He had to face down the get-you.

The monster lived in a dark wood with a brick road running through it, yet the trees spilled into a large empty house, or mansion, made of wood, all of which was located in the attic of Mark's small house (though it was not Mark's small house, it was a different one). Mark was not there, but he could see it all: the stillness of the empty mansion unnerved him beyond comprehension. Mark walked up to the attic hatch and opened it. A wooden staircase descended from the little attic door and grew longer and longer; the staircase was impossibly long despite the small size of Mark's house. He remained in place, motionless at the base of the steps, staring into the black square opening of the hatch above. Out of the stagnant dark came the get-you's hairy fingers, tipped with long, hideously jaundiced, human-nail-like claws. Its enormous hand extended further, gripping the edge of the door, about to pull itself into Mark's reality. He could not face it, the monster was invincible, it seemed. Mark forced himself awake. When he awoke, Mark could hear Ted playing guitar. He would often play (and sometimes sing) late at night, performing his extraordinary talent for no one. Mark never complained. When Mark heard Ted's music through the wall it helped lull him to sleep, just as it had when he was a little boy. On this night, however, Ted played for a cat.

Weeks prior, a stray cat (that Ted had been feeding and letting inside since the summer) appeared to be pregnant. Male cats from all over the neighborhood had been hanging around the house, leaving behind their pungent musky traces. Mark was upset about the situation, which threatened Ted, who needed the companionship of the little cat. Mark kvetched that the cats had been copulating on the front porch, and that it was not "good." Ted retorted that it was, in fact, "good," that it was the "magic of creation," and that it was "wonderful she could experience it." Ted said that the cat was a "walk-in," or a human in a past life, who was meant to be there in cat form. Mark thought that all of the cats were indeed "walk-ins," because they were walking all over him, making his house smell like a spongey potpourri of feline sexual intercourse. But he kept that feeling to himself. He said that, bottom line, they could not take care of kittens.

Ted took the ultimatum as being symptomatic of what he considered to be Mark's mental illness, or his "magical thinking."

Ted believed Mark romanticized several aspects of his life, or what he wanted out of life, and in the process eliminated or neglected the hard realities that were either inconvenient or contradicted his magical thinking. Ted had begun acquiring an internal list of what evidence supported this thesis, the kittens were the latest addition. Many of the others were to be found in his environment.

Ted had a talent for discovering what was wrong with a place, and how foolish the people were who could not see it for themselves. What's more, they could be "in on it," he often uncovered. Ted required very specific conditions on most matters to buffer from the harshness of the environments he found himself in, which very often made life almost unlivable and justified his inertia when it came to any form of self-improvement. Ted needed a very special diet, which changed too frequently to detail. He could only wear 100% cotton, and even returned items to stores if he suspected the label was lying, since the fabric stretched a certain way, or it was scratchy, etc. He suggested this was the product of foreign companies trying to kill his country's citizenry with toxic materials. This was particularly true for Ted when he purchased plastic objects that had a volatile chemical smell, as most new plastics out of the wrapper do. Ted flipped the breaker for the overhead lighting of Mark's house in order to cut back on "dirty electricity," and so their light came from just three lamps with dim, low-powered bulbs, which made it nearly impossible for Mark to read at night. For the bathroom, they had to use a flashlight.

Ted began showering only once every few weeks to avoid excessive contact with the local water supply, which had high levels of toxins (a report showed). This made Mark complain about Ted's smell. Ted said Mark had spent too much time with his mother, so he did not know how to be around men or smell like a man. Meanwhile, Ted complained about the air outside even when the air was fresh, so he refused to vent the place by opening windows. Instead, he put a series of air filtering machines in the windows which whirred and moaned incessantly and looked hideous. Ted knew Mark appreciated a certain aesthetic, which he disliked about him as another symptom of his magical thinking. He felt somewhat vindicated whenever he could justify disrupting Mark's decor and uglify in the name of health. Moreover, the filters either brought in too little air (when the weather was hot) or too much air (when it was cold). When it was stuffy and stank with body odor, Ted said it was better than the toxic air outside. When it was cold, he said they needed the oxygen, and that the proverbial "they" were keeping oxygen levels low with weather modification devices.

The cat inevitably became pregnant, though Ted did not bring the matter up until she was clearly almost ready to give birth. Mark did some research and found out that the only way to spay the cat, so advanced in her pregnancy, was to take her to an animal shelter. At the shelter, Ted would have to formally give her up for adoption while Mark would officially sign up to adopt the cat, post operation. On the night that Mark dreamt about the get-you, it was the eve before the cat's appointment at the shelter. Ted was devastated at the thought of the cat being in pain, and shuddered at the possibility of her not making it through the procedure. He made a nest for her in a little box, cushioned with non-bleached hand towels of organic cotton. She curled up inside the box, nice and warm by a space heater in the kitchen, and then Ted played music for her. He hoped his intention would emanate through the music and comfort his feline friend, manifesting healing.

The drive to the shelter took about an hour, meandering through a steep desert canyon, with a river flowing by a train track. Large ponderosa pines stood sparsely by the riverbanks, made prominent by their years and their rarity. The drive was beautiful, but they hardly noticed. The little cat was in a little cardboard box on Ted's lap, stressed and out of sorts. Ted whispered sweet nothings to the cat and played classical music on the radio in an attempt to soothe her. When they finally reached the animal shelter, in a little town at the end of the canyon, Ted's face and voice both quivered as he signed the necessary paperwork. Mark did not understand, at first, why Ted had this twitch, but then realized that Ted was struggling to hold back tears. Mark had never seen Ted like that before.

The drive back up the canyon was somber. The classical station began to play charming and upbeat music which prompted Ted and Mark to reach for the radio simultaneously. Mark flinched his hand back to let Ted change the dial, but Ted just turned the radio off. Ted almost always had a radio playing at home, a practice he had had since Mark was a boy. But on this drive he preferred silence, or the hush of the rolling tires, punctuated by gusts of wind whipping through the canyon. The visuals of the drive, however, began to filter into focus: the snow that dulled the sharp peaks of canyon mountains, the keyhole through a jagged spire of rock, atop which a vulture sunned its open wings. The surreal forms of basalt midst a tapestry of newly thawed prairie, exposing a mosaic of muted colors. The gash in the earth that opened to an indigo sky which mirrored the fragrant waters of the river below.

"Hey, pull over a minute—I just want some fresh air," Ted said.

Surprised that Ted would ever say the words "fresh air" (let alone want some), Mark swerved down one of the few roads along the canyon that cut from the highway toward the river. It was an access road to a narrow strip of land used for cattle grazing. Closer to the water, by the fence to the pasture, Mark and Ted parked and stepped outside. They stood by the barbed wire and looked at the cows.

"Is that cow dead or dying?" Ted said.

"I think, actually, she's giving birth," Mark said, who had better eyes.

"Wow, you're right," Ted said, squinting.

They stood, quiet and motionless. A tidal wave of unpleasant-looking fluid broke from the cow, after which the calf began to emerge, in a slow struggle, from its mother's womb. And then, an untold amount of time later, the calf was at last in the world. The mother got up and licked the calf clean of the sticky remains from its dark origins within her. Standing, she passed the enormous placenta, which small birds swarmed with vigor as if they knew what to expect. The calf made its first attempts to stand, which Mark and Ted both desired to witness, but the sun was getting low and the wind grew cold.

"Well, congratulations," Ted said with a grand waving gesture. It was meant to be funny, but when Mark and Ted climbed back into the car, Mark caught a glimpse of the tears in the corners of Ted's eyes. Mark had never seen Ted like that before. They rode back to the house in silence. Ten days later they repeated the trip and came back with the little cat.

Months went by with Ted trying several types of cat food, most often discovering something wrong with the brand. That summer, about five different pet food companies later, Ted asked Mark if he could return a large bag of cat food for him.

"I don't want to be known as the return guy," Ted said.

Mark said it was too late for that, but he would do it. Mark knew the real reason was that the bag was too heavy for Ted to lift without having sciatica pain, and his back was worse off than usual. Ted gave meticulous instructions about what food to exchange it for, and how to do it. Always, these missions were needlessly complicated, mostly due to a multitude of concerns Ted had stemming from his paranoia about giving out personal information.

Ted had a long history of being described as, one could say, "tinfoil hat." But his natural paranoia grew to new heights post carbon monoxide poisoning, a paranoia that was at times debilitating for him. Mark noticed this change over their many phone conversations, and he tried to be supportive, often indulging Ted's tinfoil. But while Mark generally kept an open mind, and valued Ted's knowledge, it was nevertheless an adjustment to have Ted's tinfoil around him, in person, all day every day. More and more, Mark let slip his doubts over outlandish claims such as "better self evictions," "skins," or "dog-people." And more and more Ted began to voice his disappointment in Mark, accusing him of magical thinking. Ted said that Mark lived in a romantic world of denial and could not see the horrors that faced them. That made Mark complicit with what was "going on."

Mark returned from the store, carrying the heavy bag of cat food. Ted was on the front porch, getting some sun. Mark put the bounty by the door. Ted asked about every minute detail from the transaction to make sure it happened the way he had planned. Mark did well, but he made a foolish comment, one he regretted instantly:

"When I was in the pet food aisle I heard one of those announcements over the PA system, you know, the one that says 'security check to section B, security check to section B.'"

Mark sometimes indulged Ted's paranoid ideas, and sometimes even half bought into them, but this was poorly timed.

"They're watching us," Ted said.

"Well, I think it's an automated announcement actually."

"It might be automated but they saw you and pushed a button, maybe to intimidate you or to make the employees keep tabs on you, or both... they're watching you."

"No, Ted, come on, it's clearly just at random and automated to deter shoplifting. They don't give a rat's ass about us or our damn cat food."

"Whoa, is that magical thinking, whoa is that magical thinking."

Ted then proceeded to do what he always did when it came to conflict: he fought with truth, or what he thought was true. He told Mark what was "going on," and he told Mark that he was too old not to face reality, that he needed to "be a man" about it. He told Mark that he never had a good male role model after he left, and that everything isn't a "bowl of cherries," as his mother would have him believe.

"Life isn't a bowl of shit either," Mark said.

"It can be, and it is for a lot of people, and it will be for us too if we're not careful."

"I have to go back into town, I have more errands to run... I want to apply for a bank loan to move forward with that business idea I told you about," Mark said.

Ted scoffed. Mark shook his head and walked to his car, parked in the drive. He opened the car door. But then, something sprang up within him. Immediately, he turned and walked back to Ted, who was still on the steps sneering up at him, amazed at Mark's complacency.

"You know, every time I try to tell you something about my life, my plans or aspirations, you put out my fire. It has been very hard for me, losing my family, having my teaching hours cut in half, and trying to survive out here... I do so much for this household, all I ask for is a little respect," Mark said.

"So now you're saying I'm violent."

"What?"

"You're saying that I don't respect you which means that I am violent towards you, which is absolutely crazy."

"Look, let's just call it sympathy, OK, I need you to have some sympathy for me."

"You've spent too much time with your mother. I'm a man, don't ask me to be sympathetic."

"Ted—"

Mark welled up with tears, which embarrassed him. He quickly turned away from Ted but then walked toward the car in a slow a dejected manner. The driver's door still hung wide open, promising transport into town where he had hoped to accomplish some improvement for his life, which now seemed useless. They weren't going to approve his loan anyway. Ted stood up and strode quickly over to Mark, lifted above his sciatica, lifted above his twinged posture. He walked through the pain and touched his stepson, he touched his only son, and said: "I'm sorry that I upset you."

Mark allowed the hug Ted struggled for. He held him without restraint and broke the tears they both had locked within.

"I love you Ted," Mark said, "…and I'm glad you're here."

"I love you too," Ted whispered.

It was the only time the two had acknowledged their love. It was their first true embrace.

"It's this fucked up world we're living in," Ted said. He took Mark's hand and wept. "You have to remember to be strong… and you are strong, Mark."

Ted wanted to say that he was proud of Mark, but he could not voice it, it was left to the soft currents of tacit understanding, like bits of newspaper blowing down the sidewalk, like a message in a bottle.

Ted had never said that he was proud of Mark, and he never did. It was not long until their masculine strength was decimated in an instant—in that moment that it no longer mattered, not to anyone. All that Ted had said became true, all the tinfoil hat material became true, and all that mattered became your "better self"—more on that later. But know that the crows were silent that day. Ted was silent that day: he went missing, and Mark never saw him again. Mark could no longer teach after that day. He became a telemarketer.

Mark made calls from 9 AM to 9 PM, six days a week. He was lucky, he was told, that he could work from home, remotely. He was lucky, he was told, that he made the sort of calls that he did—not only were jobs for his kind severely limited, but he had the esteemed privilege to raise money for the major performing arts venues of his region, such as the Opera or Ballet. This was because of his background in the humanities. Instead, he could be selling magazine subscriptions, or refrigerator warranties, or back scratchers, he was told. And it did not really matter if the telemarketers raised millions—they needed the organization more than the organization needed them, he was told.

But Mark already knew the game, he had done this job before, part time, long ago. Back then, he worked in an office. The people who worked in that little office had wandered there from all walks of life—they were a bizarre collection of souls. The storms of the rainy city hitting the building made Mark think, at that time, that like Jonah he had been swallowed up by something marine and dark. And so, in this way, Mark imagined he and the others existed like old sailors trapped in the belly of a whale, in an inert repetitious limbo of the working class. He lingered there for years. But the day did arrive when he finished his education. He began teaching. He left telemarketing and the city far behind—that is, until the day his better self showed up.

Mark called a patron whose name was Bud Hole. Yes, this poor bastard did not choose to go by Bill or Will or William, etc., he chose Bud. Mark was intrigued—either Bud was a joke or a very confused person, Mark thought. But Mr. Hole did not answer the phone, so Mark saved the contact info and, against company policy, decided he would try Bud once, daily, until he answered. Those days turned into weeks, and the weeks turned into months. And just when Mark was beginning to give up on the man, it happened: Mr. Hole finally picked up the phone. It was likely an accidental answer. There was a squeaky, whiney voice on the line, giving the impression of a strange, little, middle aged man.

"Hello?" he honked.

"Hi Bud, uh, Mr. Hole? This is Mark, Mark Naumann, calling from—"

Mark was cut off by a shaky, nervous "uhhhhhh" which then became: "y-y-you have reached, 206, 283, 46… 5…3…, please leave a message after the… beep..."

Mark knew what was going on, Bud Hole couldn't pull the wool over his eyes, at least not so easily. He resolved to wait for the "beep," and leave a "message."

Bud spit out a brief "pfft" of breath, apparently in preparation for the beep.

"Beeee-eeeee-ppp," Bud said, as accurately as he could muster.

"Hello Mr. Hole, this message is from Mark, calling on behalf of the Ballet... Let's see, uh, about five years ago you came out to see the Nutcracker, and we wanted to make sure you knew just how much we appreciated that support, Bud. Thank you."

Bud sighed.

"But, Bud, I was really calling for two reasons, and I'll try to be brief, I know that I'm speaking to your voicemail here. The first reason was again to thank you, thank you very much, for coming out to see the Nutcracker. The second reason I'm calling is—"

This was the point where Mark would typically shift into his pitch. But something told him to stop. Not to stop talking but rather to speak, really speak. Mark had a lot on his mind, and during this time he had no other audience but the man Hole, so passive aggressive in nature that he would be forced to listen.

There was a pause. Mr. Hole sighed once more.

"Hey, let me tell you something Bud," Mark said, "and you might want to put this on speaker phone, because it's going to take a minute—when you get around to checking your voicemail, that is…"

Mark cleared his throat. Bud yawned. Mark actually had no idea what he truly wanted to say. He rambled and ranted for a while, about nothing really. It was good just to speak and hear his thoughts out loud, garbled as they were. He had lived without listening to his own thoughts for far too long, he did not even know how to do it. Eventually, his speech changed into a stream of consciousness.

"...You know, it's funny to remember a time when you thought 40 was a far-off age. That summer, in my forties, it dawned on me that nothing seemed so far-off—all possible ages, all movement of time, it all seemed so close to me, so inexorably close and so meaningless... I had done so little of what I thought I would have done by 40... And I remember when, sometimes, an event in life would swell with an almost painful nostalgia, even as the event took place, before it had formed into some distinct dot on the map of my life... The nostalgia I felt was strangely sensual, but there was a bitterness to it, like the end of a sunset… And I remember the day all the people left, and how the sunset on that day bathed me in an almost preternatural light, cooling the summer heat with its teal ephemera…"

Mr. Hole snorted, as if waking from a brief nod.

"Where I lived was being described as a 'ghost town.' Dirt-devils whipped through its solitude. Everyone who hadn't metamorphosed into the dog phase of this plague had left, while a few of us beasts remained... Yet for me, the town was full of life... My shadows were immune to the dust. My shadows escorted me to that liminal space on the edges of a calendar, free of time. I could feel death, I could feel old age, I could feel youth, I could feel my presence, and it was all wrapped up in one story... My shoes were dusty, yes, but the shadows that went before me, and the shadows that lay behind me, sifted through the dust in a perfect dance... The soles were coming loose from my shoes. I imagined this dog-plague as a silly phenomenon of everyone losing the soles from their shoes—could we not walk without them, as shadows do? Perhaps not. Were we dogs without these soles? Perhaps so—er, I should say, 'paw-haps so,' get it?"

"Pfffft…"

"Anyway, I was living in the desert. Or rather, I lived on the edge of the desert-like badlands—you know this, of course, Mr. Hole, but the mountain range that divides our state down the middle creates an area of temperate, coastal rainforest to the west, and a semi-arid rain-shadow to the east. I lived on the threshold between these two worlds, in a town called Elmsburg... for nearly half the year it was hot and dry and yet the winters were cold, long, and snowy... Sometimes I would venture out farther east. I would drive out into those big badlands—it would appear so vast and barren to most, so hostile, rough, and sprinkled with thorns and goatheads. But to me, in the cushioned light of the dusk, the desert was like a velvet sanctuary. This was a rain-shadow, so it was a shadowland. My shadows were welcome there—everywhere else had rejected me in some way, for they denied my shadows, if you know what I mean... People used the word 'perfect' to describe any banal action that came through without messing up, or if a schedule aligned 'perfectly,' etc. And so, you were meant to be perfect and not shadowy... Maybe 'perfect' meant *predictable* or *convenient*... are shadows predictable or convenient?... Dog-people are neither...

Occasionally, I'd drive to this enormous reservoir, surrounded by countless little oases of ponds and small lakes. There, hundreds of miles inland from the coast, deep into shadowland, there were gulls and other seabirds, even pelicans... The pools of water and great expanse of the reservoir were like soft mirrors that reflected the blue light of early evening, and shadows. I would drive for over an hour just to catch this light, for a moment, and feel held by something tangible, though it was immaterial... The water of the huge reservoir, with her many gulls, of course made me think of the ocean. Whenever a fisherman's boat sped through, creating waves that knocked against the rocky banks, I thought of something a coworker in that little office once told me: that love, for him, had always been like who you get washed up on the beach with. As potentially pretentious as it sounds, I don't care, that's how it was for me too. All my loves were those I got tossed ashore with. I'm not so sure how much our choice comes into play. Does it even matter?"

"A-choo!"

"Gesundheit. Look, Bud, the metaphor also works in the case of my ex-wife, since that was indeed a damn shipwreck... That's a joke, kind of."

Mr. Hole sighed. Mark echoed the sudden expulsion of air.

"Bud, even people like me have a story to tell... I haven't told you much. I don't know why I've been rambling on in this annoyingly pretentious manner, I just don't get to talk this way, with anyone, not even myself... Let me get focused here... let's talk about what matters... Remember when they came to us all with those new skins? I remember when mine was freshly delivered. It had the same oddly attractive artificial scent as new shoes. It hung in my closet for weeks, its sewing kit placed macabrely underneath… I'm lucky to have this apartment, although I guess they had to house us somewhere… not all of us… Anyway, the plague affected people's lungs, as you know. But what isn't spoken of these days—or maybe it is, I don't know, without a skin-license I'm only allowed a radio and a landline—well, what probably isn't talked about is how people back then believed, truly believed, that they were turning into dogs. You'd get a cold, and sometimes it'd progress into a wheezing that produced a sound quite reminiscent of howling. In addition, people noticed odd hair growth. Then came the propaganda, and we were told that it would only get worse... It went to people's heads, they panicked...

Of course, the stores started to sell out of dog food first, then flea combs, frisbees, and chew toys. Parents bought muzzles for the kids who had been 'biters' in school. Corporations profited, naturally, selling designer collars, S&M leashes and chokers, so on and so forth. Many wanted to turn it into a 'positive,' they called it 'metamorphosis' and used the butterfly as a metaphor. 'As I metamorphose,' people would say…

I got sick, it felt like a cold to me, then I got better. I had some unusually long nose hairs, which I plucked. My wife got sick and started howling. She howled and she howled, until finally she howled all the way to her parents, many states away. They took her to one of those clinics where the people lick your wounds and she made a full recovery. Although, she does still bark on occasion, but that might just be reserved for when she talks to me… That was a joke, Bud, the barking part. And she never actually talks to me... The rest *did* happen, and I'm sure they're not telling you skin-wearers about it, so I'm telling *you*... Anyway, my wife left and didn't come back, and we were soon divorced. Not least, she took our young daughter with her, Faith…

I should remind you that no one really knew what caused the dog-people. Was it just psychological? Was it a pathogen? Was it an environmental poison? Was it a combination of factors? What was known, however, was the solution: the new skins… Yes siree-Bud, everyone was sold on the production of these new skins—wear them and you'll be human again. Er, I mean 'hu-an,' as they call it now. The same rhetoric was employed each time it was mentioned in the media—these skins were made by science, and 'I believe in science,' people would say ('science' became faith-based). Not much else was ever said about the skins to qualify their usage, other than the scare tactics that without them you'd turn into a dog, or worse, you'd turn our children into dogs...

Yep, Mr. Hole, they say that knowledge is power, but what I found was that acting like you know what you're talking about is even more powerful, and we were all sold a vacuum cleaner, so to speak... And each day more and more of us got sucked up into it... *believing* became more important than facts, and *knowing* became more important than knowledge...

In what we jokingly refer to as the 'before times,' though it's not so funny... Um, in the before times, we tried to escape the already advancing tidal wave of ugly Americanism... I guess when I say 'we' I mean *me*, and those who already had the dog in us, I suppose... Anyway, I tried to deny what I like to call the 'strip-mall dynamo.' I thought I had sought refuge in Elmsburg but when the dog-plague hit I was like a snarling beast pushed into a corner... and then the day came when all the beasts fell silent, suburbia roared like a freeway, and no one dares speak of tearing it down…

Ugly Americanism used to be the enemy, but then came the day when being ugly was being beautiful... After our better selves showed up and evicted the dogs, a suburban hell ripped through our valley with a lava flow of construction... I hear it's just nothing but cookie-cutter housing and fast food now, and of course people are seen as 'beautiful' for eating fast food now. You can't say that fast food is unhealthy anymore..."

Mark did not include everything. He did not say everything he wanted to. He did not, for example, mention how it had all happened. He did not express the undercurrent of yearning that he had lived with for so many years, ripping his sense of presence away from him, frantically shooing his consciousness into a metaphysical waiting room where he waited for his real life to arrive. There, on the lounge tables of this waiting room, were piles of magazines picturing dreams, "the American Dream," or the imagery of living close to one's dream—being their "better self," many would say...

The new skins were marketed as a way for people to not only stay hu-an but to become their "better self." The skins were required, of course. Each adult received a new skin by post, along with sewing kits—it was somehow painless, and the skin would retain your "hu-anity." There were no ill-effects, it was claimed. Those who sewed on the skins became bona fide citizens, with a license. Those who refused became less than second class—they were seen as dogs, even if they had not yet "metamorphosed" (actually, the folks that had created the "metamorphosis" axiom soon abandoned their terms, moved on to other word-wars, and acted as if it was never even said... it became "revolutionary" or "cool" to sew on the new skin). Those who refused lost their jobs. Mark lost his.

Mark also lost his home, which happened to most in his position. He did not understand it, but his better self showed up anyway one day—when Mark returned from the pet store, his better self was there, sitting on his couch in the living room. Immediately, his better self stood up and effortlessly threw Mark out of the house, without a word. Mark did not understand it—maybe the skin that hung in the closet took on a shape of its own? Or perhaps, worst of all, Mark had traded places. That is to say, perhaps Mark became the skin—an empty bag of skin, thrown to drift with the breeze down the curb of hu-anity like an inflated piece of garbage. His refusal transformed him into refuse. That was the day Ted left too. Mark did not see it happen but Ted's better self showed up first. And, without any sciatica, he chased Ted into the prairie wasteland, full of goatheads. The cat left, slept under a neighbor's porch, and mournfully missed Ted to the end of her days. Ted's better self drove south to work for a storage company. A murder of crows circled a bag of skin in the desert but did not utter a sound. Ted would not have known what that meant.

Mark slept in his old car for a few days (he noticed his better self had a new car, a standard domestic car; adequately modern, rewardingly normal). However, Mark did manage (once) to break into his house. He had but a moment, so he could only take a shoebox full of photos, as well as a few books, and a few odds and ends. These were things his better self did not care for, so it did not much matter anyway. At night, in the back of his car, he looked through the photo-memories. Shadows were cast across the pictures, by the light of a streetlamp. Shadows crept back into his consciousness. His memories were shadows. His family was a shadow. He was an empty bag full of shadows—or was it ashes? The smoke still gushed into the valley from nature's funeral pyre on the hills and mountains. Maybe those ashes filled him. Or maybe it was the ashes of his own past, incinerated beyond utterance: it was painful to face but he had had a family, including his daughter, Faith.

She was only a toddler when they left. Mark thought of how shadows already affected her life. Mark remembered a time that he had lost his temper and yelled at Faith to stop doing something (he could not even remember what it was). She cried. He said he was sorry. He held her. Then he noticed a favorite stuffed animal wedged behind the couch, one they thought was lost forever. He handed it to her and she took the toy rapidly. She put it under her arm and tried to quell her own tears with a self-soothe. In his memory, it seemed to Mark that this toy was like a little bag, which Faith carried under her little arm, in which her papa had put a little shadow. He wept. He missed her more than he could express, and all he had were these photos and memories.

But Mark was soon found by the police. His car was confiscated and he was moved into some miserable and miniscule housing in the city; a building with a chain-link gate, much like a kennel. There he caught a stomach illness. Only a veterinarian doctor would see him, who gave him a dewormer. Mark thought he had just eaten something undercooked, since all he could buy were raw meat byproducts with rice and peas, from the pet food store (dogs were not allowed in the regular grocery stores, since it violated health regulations). He never took the dewormer. Mark felt better after about a week.

"...One summer, I took a job in my hometown driving a taxi... It was alright... Typically, I'd either drive tourists to see a lavender farm with an expensive giftshop, or to the beach, or I'd drive the same old locals to the same destinations, and always at the same times—small town people can be creatures of habit. One such local was a younger man, extremely soft spoken, one you couldn't imagine ever raising his voice let alone possessing a temper of any kind. But, he had been a soldier, back just a few years since the war. He worked as an insulator. He told me a little about the combat he saw. It was horrific, though highly mechanized. He came under frequent fire from an enemy that was not even physically present— the weapons were remote, set to timers. He lost much of his hearing. His eyes were always distant. 'But I don't have that in me anymore,' he said. 'Now I just do insulation.'… I started to think, back then, that even our most valorous attempts in this world were thrown to the far more insidious violence of something automated and impersonal. We didn't have any real fight in us. Our only protection was what could insulate us psychically… Maybe that's part of what went wrong with my marriage… Maybe we're living in a world where people don't fall in love anymore… I don't think people do, and these skins are just the physical manifestation of the mental insulation we've been installing for years and years and years… Who falls in love wearing those skins? Do you love anyone, Mr. Hole?"

Bud hiccupped out of nervousness.

"Excuse me. I am forgetting this is just your voicemail… I was never able to insulate myself. I was sensitive to the cold, I was sensitive to the sharp collisions between myself and Evelyn.

Particularly when we were with her family: oft a well-funded period of recreation, such as annual reunions somewhere tropical. And it was always immediately prior to an episode of 'fun' in which she'd strip me of my armor... I mean to say, she would want to clash with me as soon as my guard was relaxed in anticipation of said fun... I'd naturally (and profoundly) lean into her criticisms, and then I'd just tag along. I'd join the fun... Usually there was some small novelty involved with their moments of fun... like... a Pink Cadillac margarita... Yes, I remember—it was one of a number of instances that have all morphed together... staring into that Pink Cadillac margarita, sinking into its exhausting irony... I became like the salt crystals on the edge of the glass, dissolving into careless lime—the shards of our intimacy didn't matter to anyone but myself. Just so long as I didn't get in the way of a good time. It forced me to be out of my body and watch someone else be present... It wasn't me... I suppose it was my better self who had usurped my presence, even then—perhaps taking me for a test drive, and it was only a matter of time until he showed up for good... I'd watch myself imitate the fun people were having, but from a far away perch I was still looking into the abyss of my Pink Cadillac margarita."

Mark also told Bud Hole that all the fairy tales were untrue. Ted was right. He had learned that their magic was false, and no fairy had any substance in the world. All except for the big bad wolf, he was real. And those who wore the skins were like a wolf in hu-an's clothing, who huffed and puffed and blew the lonely dog houses in. The big bad wolf blew gusts that whipped the dogs in the eyes and made them wince into the lachrymose of oblivion. And the big bad wolf's howl silenced all music. All that was left of music was a dumb thumping discordant mess of sound. Most people forgot what music was even like. They held onto the few threads of melody that would occasionally appear, like scraps leftover from the past banquet of human emotion. These threads would sometimes catch someone, alone, with no other sensation, numbed beyond their skins—these scraps would touch the edges of their contact with the old earth, and they would sing the one iota of harmony that affected them, as a symphony had once done to others in the "before times."

Visual art was being dismantled as well. Art was garbage. It actually began several years prior, when Mark was working for theatres and venues in the city. The municipal government tore down the old Opera House in order to build a "modern" performance hall. "Better acoustics" was the primary selling point to the public. The old Opera House was built in a very classic style, with intricate chandeliers hanging in the foyer, commanding the audience to attempt some modicum of elegance in their appearance. The new hall that replaced the Opera House was indeed better in its acoustics, but it was bare and insipid. The old chandeliers were replaced by chandeliers made of found objects: vacuum cleaners, dusters, plastic ferns, calculators, folding chairs, lamps, egg cartons, and so on. Those who attended felt more comfortable, Mark was told. Under the new lights those who donated thousands to the Opera or Ballet (patrons who were part of the "director's circle," or "members of the barre") could now wear track suits and ripped jeans. It was also "inclusive," Mark was told. In his office they would joke and call the new lights the "hanging garbage of Babylon," or "garbageliers." Mark would add to the joke and say that it wasn't art, it was "fart."

Shortly before the dog-plague hit, in his little prairie town, Mark walked past the local art gallery, the epicenter of art in the region, and noticed there was a highly advertised exhibit from a highly celebrated artist. He peeked through the windows. To his astonishment, it seemed that the installation was nothing more than an old couch with some garbage strewn about it, slightly arranged. The exhibit was touted as "brilliant." It brought to life the living rooms of "real people," or so they said. The chandelier that had become a garbagelier was then deconstructed into just plain garbage, placed in a room with some sort of order. A year later, however, soon after the dog-plague came, that same art gallery showcased a black plastic bag, full of garbage. It was in the center of the room. It represented the "erasure" of people by "toxic masculinity," or men who "invalidated" those peoples' garbage. Your garbage (if you were not a certain type of male) was "amazing." Your refuse (if you wore the skin) made you "amazing." It was "perfect." Many things were "perfect." Accomplishing the most mundane of tasks would illicit the "perfect" response from others—if you wore a skin, that is. For example, if you gave a waiter your credit card when the bill came, they praised it as "perfect."

A year further down the road of dog-plague, the exhibit became an *empty* garbage bag, without purposeful placement. The bag got kicked to the edge of the room and covered in the dust that drifted in from outside. Art had finally become "fart," as Mark called it. But then like any gas, it dissipated into the ether, and the bag deflated. Mark had deflated. He was this bag, on the edge of the room, while the room was crowded with so-called patrons (*i.e.* filled by those who validated themselves and each other; by people who were "perfect;" by people who were their better selves).

In the good old days, Mark did much better at promoting the arts. He sold countless subscriptions over the phone, and procured countless little donations. But in the plague-days, Mark did not do so well. Of course, it was partly the fault of the supposed "leads." Back when, Mark would primarily contact actual subscribers and donors, people who possessed some proximity of time to the campaign at hand. Now with the Ballet, for example, he only called folks who had gone to the Nutcracker, years and years ago.

But it was also more than that. Mark did not exactly believe in what he was selling either. Without a skin-license, he was not allowed to attend the Ballet, or Opera, or any venue. So it did not much matter. Though he knew what was being performed no longer held any appeal for him anyway. He had no wish to exclude others, but he preferred to remember a few years of excellence, before operas showcased tone-deaf divas, before musicals were restricted to rap that did not rhyme, and before ballerinas had a 150 kilo minimum requirement for hire.

Though, for some time even before the plague, it had been difficult for most people to face their inadequacies, or their shadow-selves. Which is why most of the people who lived in Mark's state resided to the west of the mountains, away from the rain-shadow, where the pouring rain washed away their bullshit and kept them indoors to waste countless hours. That is likely the reason why, as Mark had noticed in the before times, whenever folks visited Elmsburg for the first time (from what they called the "westside") they often had a bit of an existential crisis, confronted with a stark bereft landscape closely adjacent to their lush green expanse they just assumed went on forever. But with the dog-plague came a reason to never visit anywhere like Elmsburg again, to leave it as a steaming pile of fast food, and a reason to usher-in a great celebration of inadequacy.

Video games, for example, were considered good for your mental health, especially if you let it parent your children for half the day (or full days on the weekend). Video games improved cognition for youth in the realms of "impulse control" and "attention;" the *new* studies (to *reproduce* results no longer mattered in science, only what was *new*) recommended at least six hours of video games per day for every child.

The great celebration of inadequacy also included the wearing of the skins themselves, and it was tied into social justice somehow. That is to say, if you just simply wore a skin you were acting as a "social justice warrior"—that is really all it took, and if you did not wear a skin you were bigoted somehow. Well, *some* people did do a *little* more than that. For instance, it became popular for a white person to put a social justice sign in their apartment window, and so the city became a billboard smorgasbord of messages only white people would endorse (*e.g.* "racism: enough is enough"). Moreover, people's inadequacies were seen as further evidence of their perfection.

The "warrior" in "social justice warrior" should be emphasized here: simultaneous to the dog-plague, a big country, far away, invaded a little country next to it. The little country had long been a cesspool of corruption and organized crime, and it had a poor track record for hu-an rights. But because it was a *little* country, the skin-people supported it and their government gave incredible amounts of money to the little country's resistance fighters. None of the skins went to fight in the war, they were too busy playing video games, but they wanted their government to give the little country lots of money and weapons. The big country (who was much like the little country, just bigger) threatened to use nuclear bombs if the resistance did not end. Because the little country was, in fact, a little country, the skins thought that what had been described by their president as imminent "nuclear Armageddon" was "worth it," and so they kept supporting the war and kept playing video games.

To be oppressed had become for the skins both sacred and a hot commodity. Indeed, their own country simply gave the little country ammunitions and then printed the cash difference, put into the pockets of self-proclaimed diplomats. So, it made lots of money for people to not like oppression. About ten percent of the Earth soon became uninhabitable due to the atomic blasts that followed, and the little country became part of the big country anyway, but it was all "worth it." All facts to the contrary became filtered through this narrative and so disregarded as "misinformation." The war was also the fault of the dogs, somehow. And to at all criticize the little country in anyway, or to even mention the severity of the nuclear fallout, was taboo and dog-like. Nuclear issues were perpetuated by oppressors and colonizers, somehow. Only dogs thought otherwise, only dogs had those opinions. Moreover, opinions were like a dog's asshole, as people would say in response to any contrasting idea. And dogs were seen too as colonizers, somehow.

Pop-music stars, who had become wonderfully fat, would shake their planetary sized asses in a hypnotic frenzy known as "twerking" and then pause to give a brief and wholly unrelated salute to social justice, typically uttering a single word that was trending in the moment, what people called "viral." One such viral word that buzzed at the time was "boom," which referenced the bombs everyone wished would fall in the war the little country fought with the big country, though the irony was that most of the bombs that blew up did so in retaliation against the little country. But that fact was too nuanced for most people to understand.

There were many other viral words that floated around and won the spotlight between the giant gyrating butt cheeks of popstars, mostly starting with the letter "b," including "booboo," "buns," "blur," "beep," "bop," "bang," and so on. These viral words were often the only words uttered at all by the popstars, who no longer sang, they just shook their huge asses to electronic drumbeats and shrill ambulance-siren-like whistling tones. Mark thought what was "viral" was more virulent than the so-called dog virus. But that was just his opinion. Opinions were like a dog's asshole.

Granted, most dog-people, when not too hungry or weak to think, in fact did *not* support the war. But their opinions did not matter, or rather, their opinions were toxic. It was considered toxic to offer strong opinions for *anything* other than the consensus thought, which offered set terms and canned rhetoric to yell (at the appropriate moments) in order to combat oppression (mostly virtual "yelling" on social media platforms over a virtual network called the "internet;" activism that was proudly thought of as "virtual/virtue-all" activism). And people were constantly connected to their virtual platforms (or being what was called "online") without breaks.

Nor could one "fixate" on any topic of conversation for too long (or for more than 30 Mississippis before becoming toxic, as a new study showed). In addition, people felt, *en masse*, that "toxic masculinity" was the great invalidator. And everyone who mattered was invalidated in some way by "toxic masculinity." Naturally, connections were soon drawn between the psychological pathogen of "toxic masculinity" and contracting the actual plague. Doctors in the public eye, or those who held office, claimed that the great invalidator degraded your immune system and, in effect, made you vulnerable to the plague. Theorists posited that the "alpha" and "pack mentality" of "toxic masculinity" was perhaps even the main culprit of the dog-plague's bizarre nature.

The heinous miasma of "toxic masculinity" of course lurked in men, but due to the patriarchal system, it could be found in all corners of society. It was necessary to clean it up. The first societal line of defense against this invisible foe was to screen men (and then, later, all people) for any signs of invalidating behavior. Training to this end was given in the workplace. The primary thing one learned from being trained (it was also known as being "tamed") was to not openly dislike anything that others liked. This especially applied to video games, television shows, cartoons, movies, sports, and popular music. Moreover, one was encouraged to like what everyone else liked. "Fake it until you make it," they would say at training sessions. People learned to respond to things they did not care for with "that's really interesting," or "thanks for sharing, I'll have to look into that," or "that's cool." The second line of defense was the skin-wearing mandate. Those who refused to wear the new skins were seen as both dogs *and* complicit with "toxic masculinity." The people who did not wear the skins were like bulls in a China shop, anything they touched in society could break, could wear down the immune system, could break down hu-anity itself. The great invalidators became the invalids...

"...But I felt like an invalid long before... I learned over many years that you can't fit everything neatly into one place. You can't put all of your eggs into one basket... Not that I have any eggs left to spare... I dream of eggs, sizzling in butter, I can't get them anymore... We had a chicken coop once—no, *I* had a chicken coop. My wife made that clear, and she didn't enjoy the attention I gave the chickens. Sometimes she claimed to 'hate' them. And yet, other times, she would 'love' them. Her hate stemmed from any distraction away from her, while her love came from moments the chickens could be used as a way to place her in the spotlight: a photograph with a chicken for social media, a novelty to show dinner guests... I thought that perhaps her love required extreme dedication. But then my pledge of allegiance called her bluff—her love, her hate, any severe emotion she subscribed to was a bluff, a puff of air, mere words spoken because she knew that they were words one said when certain cards were on the table. Her poker exterior was impenetrable, and emotions had to be choreographed... She pretended to be fragile, but she really had a thick skin... The skin she wore was superfluous, it only covered an invisible callous that had contained and protected her hu-anity for decades. She howled those last days with me because she thought that she was supposed to howl, and so she howled, for as long as she thought she *should* be howling."

Bud Hole belched loudly. "Excuse me, oh—" he said.

"That's alright. I don't want to sound as though we shared nothing. But I'm finding it difficult to separate my fantasies of what we shared from reality, mirage from oasis, water from sand… So it is that I don't even know what we shared, though I fell into a sort of despair over losing what we shared… But this wound was more than personal. I felt as though the loss was final—not just for us. For me, for everyone—it was as if we all had sand in our mouths. There was no love left, anywhere. Love was only either a bluff at cards or a choreographed routine—it was planned, it was an appropriate set of predictable actions, it was a reflection of societal compliance… Us beasts tend to think of love as coming from the earth, and it is only civilization that covers the earth. It's been this way for as long as anyone can remember… In old romantic novels, sad beasts who lost their lover to, say, 'consumption,' would sneak into the grave and lay beside their corpse. Scheming and plotting their plot in death to touch their love's own resting place—being buried together, decomposing together, becoming earth together, was what love was. Now we are only buried alone, if we are buried at all—a lack of space means more cremation, more dusts scattered to the wind, more sand in our mouths. And they dare not bury the dog-people, so we don't even have the earth to return to… The loss of love was final— our loves have all died of consumption, but it is societal consumption, a societal vacuum, and society leaves no trace, no remains, not even in death…

I did see her again, only once. It was by accident, yet also possessed some intentionality, as if we were both wandering around the same room with our eyes closed, waiting to bump into each other... She was traveling in the area, and was shopping for her Dachshund. Our daughter Faith wasn't there, so I assumed she was with her grandparents... I should mention that in the pet-supply store, the skins who come to shop for their pets are always extremely nervous—it shows, even through their dermatological adornment. They know that the dog-people also shop there. Evelyn was no exception, I saw how apprehensive she was. But what was perhaps Evelyn's worst fear she did not fully realize until it stood facing her: me...

She looked horrified, studying my change... I did not think that I had changed. I have only ever been myself. But she traced each minutia of my being with a fine-toothed comb in order to verify the dog in me. A flea comb, you could say. Every twitch, every blink, every breath was stitched into a narrative, like a loud infomercial, advertising the beast. To her I didn't really exist, so she hadn't expected me. For Evelyn, the dog had devoured me long ago. And with me, the beast had swallowed her memory of me, or suffocated the light cast upon me in her mind. I was then only a shadow for her, crouched in the two dimensional prison that stuck to the walls of her subconscious.

'Eve,' I said.

'I shouldn't be speaking with you,' she said. I stepped closer to her, with feeble tenderness. She took a step back.

'I signed the documents and sent them to you, did you get them?'

'Yes, Mark, but I don't think that matters anymore, not with the new laws in place,' she said.

Evelyn sighed, as she had done, countless times before; a specific sort of sigh that was customary to our marriage…

'Here I am talking to you, and I shouldn't be,' she said. 'You still have not learned to listen to me.' She sighed again. The familiarity of her sigh, though it commanded a sense of urgency within me, was nevertheless comforting. It was something I could hold onto, a small detail that was particular to us, and so oddly intimate.

'Eve, can we please talk?'

'I don't know Mark, I don't think we can. I don't think it's safe.'

'I don't live in a safe world, I don't care.'

'Not for you, maybe, but you might want to consider what talking to you might do to me. I can't open up these wounds, I can't relive my trauma… do you want the vociphalitis to return? And what about our daughter, Mark? It could spread to her… you only think of yourself, that's why you've become what you are, you did it to yourself, but you have no accountability, as per usual.'

'Vociphalitis?'

'You don't even know—why am I not surprised? The howling, Mark, the howling.'

'I'm fine, I'm healthy, I'm not going to make you howl.'

'Even if you don't reinfect me directly, you are toxic to me, and that toxicity can lead to relapse—don't you listen to the news?'

'No.'

'Your ignorance is a privilege.' Eve huffed and looked at the time on her mobile phone, then looked up and to her left, toward the ceiling. In a way, the look was akin to rolling her eyes, though rather than pure annoyance it expressed being in a hurry, and that Mark was wasting her time. Eve had learned in her academic circles that people in power asserted their power through their expression of time.

'Shouldn't the skin you wear protect you?'

'There are "skin-break" cases, some people are still being infected.'

'So the skin is worthless—'

'No, Mark, it's not, those cases are very rare—I can't believe what you're saying—'

'So, if the skin does work, just speak with me for a few minutes, come on Eve.'

'…we can't talk here.'

We moved to her car. She drove, with me hiding in the back, to a small parking lot behind a wall of trees. The fall foliage of the trees was something I had not experienced in a long while. Leash laws prevented me from going to the park, and the city cut down all of the trees along sidewalks in an attempt to prevent the dog-people from publicly urinating. (Fire hydrants, however, remained an issue). The leaves of the shrub-like trees, planted in an unnaturally tight and ordered unit, were from a world I was so deprived of that they appeared sensuously resplendent.

'OK, we can talk here, no one should be around right now, but stay in the back just in case.' She kept her eyes forward, looking out for others—it was a good excuse not to look at me.

'How is Faith?'

'She's fine, she's with her grandparents while I'm here for this conference.'

'You're presenting at a conference?—and, they have her by themselves?'

'What did you want to talk to me about, Mark?'

'Perhaps it doesn't matter, the paperwork is null and void, since I have no rights.'

'So, you're wasting my time and being selfish, how typical of you.'

'The documents you can shred, you can toss them, but let's think for a moment of what we're throwing away—it's more than a piece of paper going into the rubbish bin.'

Evelyn sighed, but this sigh was different, it was unfamiliar. Those simple words I had said moved her sternum, as if dog fangs had been carried on my breath and punctured through her chainmail armor, through her tough exterior, through that skin she wore. I saw the change and whispered that she look at me. She closed her eyes and leaned forward, shaking her head slowly. A grimace appeared, she was in real pain—a pain that was shared between us, a pain I lived with every day. She winced, about to shed genuine tears. The skin that seemed to be worn so lightly was now heavy and burdensome.

'Eve, please look at me,' I said. Tears soft as a fine dust, as gentle as the ashes in our bags, flowed down my whiskers. She turned to face me, finally. And I saw her, I saw her as she was, it was as if the skin she wore did not exist... And she saw me, she saw me as I was, it was as if the dog did not exist... I touched her sweet shoulder and we both did our best to smile... We loved each other, in that moment, and nothing else mattered."

Bud expelled some annoyance in an exhale that separated his lips abruptly.

"Yes, Bud, in an instant it was over, poof, gone. The glimmer of our bond fell back down the hole... Her skin reappeared, the dog returned, and I saw her eyes fade back into a forward glance...

'We don't work,' she said through lingering tears. Then the tears vanished like a magic trick. 'I just hurt you, and you *really* hurt me... it can't work Mark, it just can't.'

And then we were gone from each other, left to curl up on each of our lonely mattresses, like crumpled wads of paper drifting down the garbage void. And all possible contracts that could be made between anyone else blew down the street with the lost words of yesterday's newspapers, real estate open house pamphlets, expired coupons, and so on."

Back in the days when Evelyn had left with Faith, many others also fled from the town. The majority of those who stayed behind were the howlers: people who were either beyond the help Evelyn had acquired or, like Mark, immobilized by something ineffable, like the poltergeist who cannot leave the confines of its haunting. There was a railroad that ran freight across the valley, into the sunset, and so cut down the center of town, which was not far from Mark's home. Whenever the train whistle blew, a plagued chorus of howls reverberated through the neighborhood, issuing from forgotten crags and dark places, where the dogs resided. It became known as "dog town." But it was also a "ghost town," and those dogs who remained were the ghosts, and their "boo" was the howl, echoing through the vacant streets, drifting with the desert ennui of tumble weeds.

Mark would sometimes wander by the old train station, which had long been forgotten and abandoned by the commuter since well before the plague hit. The station was then all but empty besides one back-corner room, occupied by a semi-retired real estate agent (rarely ever there). The left wing of the station was for a time a mattress store, though by then vacant—so vacant one would never know it had ever been there. Mark would shuffle silently, as ghosts do, around the old building and peer into its windows. He truly could not imagine the life that once bustled there, he could not feel any of it, nor any lingering presence. The station had lived with emptiness for so long that not even ghosts could fill it. The people who moved their frenetic lives by the mechanical rhythms of the place had since completely lost touch, and no energy persisted. Mark felt nothing. He sensed only the vacuous dimensions of the building. Mark wondered if he, then, would disappear as these ghosts had.

Eventually, however, came the day when the people returned to Elmsburg. The town was no longer described as a "ghost town" or "dog town." But then, Mark was not a person. He was given the skin to wear to become a person, but he could not do it. He was a dog. And then he learned to prefer the loneliness of a ghost, it was more bearable than the loneliness of a dog. The ghost that faded into obscurity was forgotten, perhaps lost. The dog was purposefully dehumanized, and so ushered violently into isolation. And he was still a dog.

Mark did not remember (so he did not mention it to Mr. Hole) that in the store where he had met Eve a song piped in over the intercom. The radio Mark had at home only picked up a few signals. Mark thought that the radio itself was faulty, since it was a cheap government loaner. But actually, there were just a handful of stations that remained on the dial, and they never aired "music." The rest of the radio was static, like an electric hush, like an electric boot softly crushing the fallen leaves of culture. So it was rare for Mark to hear a song.

The tune that played in the pet food shop was a recent hit called "Summa," sung by a female artist who called herself "Vanny del Nuys." She was considered a "genius" because she sang lyrics that she supposedly wrote herself, and she was considered "amazing" just for singing at all. Moreover, the song was highly celebrated for its use of an actual musician, called "Pappy Punk," who played the "trashcan harp" on his head (an urban instrument that had acquired some mainstream popularity). The hook in her new song (and only intelligible part) went something like this: "summa, it's summa, summa summa summa, and it's sad sad, summa summa sad sad, summa summa sad sad sad." But to hear these simple words spoken in conjunction with some iota of melody was enough to nearly bring Mark to tears, it had been so very long. Then he overheard a small gathering of people next to him:

"Oh my god, Dale, what is it?"

"Huh?"

"I thought you were like looking at your phone or something but you're just staring into space like a creep."

"I'm listening to the song."

"Uh-oh, guys, he has that smart look in his eyes."

"His smart look?"

"Oh my god, he's so smart, yesterday he like literally fixed the toilet on his own."

"I mean, I just plunged it."

"Whoa, you guys have a plunger? Where do you even buy that?"

"I found it online."

"So, Dale, what's this smart look about?"

"Well, I'm listening to the song and, uh, I think I know what it's about."

"See, smart look."

"What's it about then, smarty pants?"

"Well, I think that it's summer, it's summer time and, well, it's sad, it's a sad time, and I think maybe she's sad too." There were gasps of awe. "I mean, I know that it's art and open to interpretation, but that's what I get out of it anyway."

"Oh my god guys, that's nothing—Dale, tell them about the heater!"

"Oh no, Dale, what did you do with a heater?"

"Well, for a while it was really hot in my office, and all I ever heard from people complaining about it was that there was something wrong with the heating system. And it was the dead of winter too, so people would be bundled up like Nanook of the north, enter the floor where our cubicles are, and just immediately sweat bullets—I called them 'cube-icicles,' you know, to be *ironic*."

"Oh my god, such big words!"

"People bought individual electric fans, had a pair of flip-flops by their desk to change into, even shorts. Hawaiian shirt day became every day."

"So, what happened?"

"Well, for weeks people suffered. They'd complain, they'd moan, they'd look up at the air ducts and ask 'why?' Then, one night, I had to go in late and work on something that had an approaching deadline. The elevator was being used by the custodians for something, so I had to take the stairs. I walked up *eleven floors*, in my winter clothes, so I was already boiling by the time I got to my office. I walk in and the heat hits me like a brick wall. I make a fast move to shed my heavy coat but, right at the top, the zipper gets stuck."

"Oh my god."

"Why didn't you just pull the coat off over your head?"

"Yeah, I tried that, but I had so many layers on that I couldn't get my arms up high enough, I was totally stuck."

"Oh my god."

"I panicked, I squirmed and yelled, and flung about in desperation. I became severely short of breath and thought I would pass out from sheer heat exhaustion. That's when, from the perspective of one of my spastic contortions, I saw it—it had been evading everyone for days and days on end, yet suddenly there it was—"

"What?"

"The thing I think they call a 'thermostat.'"

"Fascinating."

"So, so, what did you do?"

"Well, I walked up to it. Heaving and faint, I steadied myself by leaning on the wall and took a good long look at the thing. I noticed, at length, that there were two buttons, each in the shape of an arrow, one pointing down, the other pointing up. I pressed on the arrow that pointed down and, go figure, the temperature went down too. I kept at it until I found a comfortable temperature. And that's how it is, to this day."

"Oh my god, you're amazing."

Mark moved away. Mark was freezing cold. Most people who wore skins also wore light, loose clothing, except in the most frigid of weather. The skins gave people extra warmth, so across the nation AC units were reinstalled and reset to compensate, with the ability to sync to mobile devices (miniature computers with tiny screens that were mostly used to stay online for social media purposes, as well as applications that performed some random function like that of a thermostat—sometimes these devices were also used as a phone). This was done by a large subsidized corporation, and it was easier to replace the entire units than teach the public about thermostats and indoor heat regulation—physical buttons had become such a scarce presence. But this plan backfired, as people were constantly competing over the desired temperature— whoever had the fastest thumbs in the office or home became the master of the AC. Each office and home had its own "fastest thumbs in the west" hu-an. (It took a while to update all the units, and obviously, Dale's office was such an example). In addition, the skins restricted a wide range of movements—it could have been that Dale was not able to pull his coat over his head not so much because he wore a sweater under his coat but because his skin prevented him from doing so. Therefore, it did not much matter that Ballerinas had to be at least 150 kilos, since the skins already stopped them from lifting their legs or arms very high. But appearances became everything. And judging people based on their skin became everything. Mark still had plug-in fans and space heaters, which were government loaners, and people saw him as a dog. He was "dog-presenting."

Mark drew in a breath of air to tell Bud Hole this last bit of his story, but there was dead air on the other end. Bud had finally hung up. Mark leaned his ear onto the landline receiver and rested in the momentary wane of time, waiting for some sense of comfort or resolve to come through the phone. But nothing happened. He felt nothing. He only thought about his hometown, and he wanted to go home.

Mark grew up on an island. During most of his childhood, the isle was known for not being very well known. However, by the time Mark was an adult, the island had turned into an overdeveloped destination, abundant with opulent vacation homes and large gated "communities." There had always been somewhat of a disparity between the rich and poor, but until that fateful transition in demographics, it had never quite been all that blatant. Once upon a time, the island held onto a general appearance of *genuine* community, and with it an understanding that income had little to do with one's dignity. Though, certainly, wealthy people had always lived on the island (even in winter), the lion's share of the year-round population was working or middle class. But, as the years passed, this dynamic changed more and more, until the breaking point—which was punctuated, severely, by one particular instance.

Mark had a friend he went through all grades with, called Ryan. They were not very close friends, but they were friendly enough. And this was not unusual: Ryan was an extremely likeable character and an all-around nice kid, so outside of his typical circle of friends he had many other minor friendships and acquaintances. He had thick curly dark brown hair that responded wildly to the slightest wind, like thousands of static bolts shooting off a plasma globe. He had wide-framed round glasses, did not have the best of posture, and wore a persistent smirk with a mischievous aura (although he was so mild mannered and good tempered that it was only the product of his well-developed sense of humor). Mark and Ryan would walk to school together, since they lived in the same neighborhood. For Mark, Ryan was a pleasant and familiar presence that was simply a staple of his childhood—he took Ryan for granted, as did his peers, because Ryan was as reliable as spring daffodils. But that aforementioned change brewed slowly: more and more well-off students went to school on the island, and with them, all of their entitlement.

Mark always thought of his hometown as a sort of Eden, and decades later he was not quite sure why he ever left. What Mark forgot was that, at the time, his exodus was the result of the island's "send forth our youth" attitude, causing him and others to think they were destined for great things on the mainland. Really, their departure was the byproduct of a disintegrating community, and what happened to Ryan could not have reflected this more. The island-Eden Mark thought of so many years later (with its pristine waters, seals, deer, dark green forests, and foxes) was coveted by a bourgeois elite who had no intention of planting generational roots in the place. Young people belonged off the island.

Ryan did not have a car, but he had a bike. He was 18 at the time. Despite his less than perfect posture, Ryan's biking skills were excellent: as a teen he pedaled his way for miles and miles around the island, conquering its many hills. That summer, however, he had graduated to a motorized bicycle and tore off down the country lanes at 30 miles an hour. Actually, the new bike was a downgrade: earlier that year, Ryan had been caught driving after having a few beers with his high school chums. He had been made "an example" by the community: the island threw the book at him, so to speak, determined to "make him responsible"—particularly the arresting deputy sheriff, Officer D. Tish, who gave a harsh testimony. Ryan barely made it through the legal hoops that ensued, and he was devasted at the thought of letting so many people down, people who had regarded him as a "good kid." So, for his transportation, Ryan fell back on his talent as a cyclist.

Perhaps Ryan's recent "mistake" was the manifestation of a subconscious wish to remain in the community and not join the diaspora of his peers, despite his dreams of becoming a filmmaker—Ryan had such a deep connection to the place, far more than most, and if anyone belonged to the island it was him. Who knows, but either way he had not yet moved off the island. He was working as a bagger at the local "Queen's Market" grocery store, and was saving for California and a life working in cinema.

Ryan was downtown and about to bike home from work when he ran into his mother. She told him, in a very routine and loving way, that she would see him at home, and to "be careful." A few months prior, she had lost her husband, who had died after a long struggle with cancer, so she told her son to be careful often. She knew how precious he was. Ryan gave his little smile, though he was slightly annoyed (as any teenager would be) and thumbed the lotto ticket he had just purchased for reassurance (it was placed neatly in his pocket and made him feel like an adult). Then he biked off. Ryan's mother went down to the docks to keep a date with some friends at "Canary Row," a restaurant overlooking the water.

As Ryan's mother walked in through the heavy doors with kitschy brass handles in the shape of salmon, Jennifer exited the building. Near the dining area there was (for the island) a fairly posh watering hole where Jennifer, then 21, had just spent the afternoon clinking glasses with her own mother, who left before Jennifer did. At the corner store down the block, Jennifer picked up a few cases of beer and a bottle of vodka. And pretty soon, she gathered together a small group of friends. A couple of them were younger than she, and in fact were in the same graduating class as Ryan (they knew him and liked him, as everyone did). Jennifer, meanwhile, had already left to live off the island, but she was there that summer to be with family, and to party with friends. Jennifer had that air of prestige only money can buy (though truly, it did not take much when compared to the island working class). When you were with her, you felt privileged, like a special member of something, like flying first class—that or you were just excluded, not on the list and so did not exist.

Jennifer tore off into the sunset with her giggling gaggle of carefully selected friends, her red car blending with the summer colors of their island at dusk—it was *their* island, after all, a VIP island, and others were a distasteful distraction from that fact. Ryan, though he was generally well liked, was still an other. He was also in the way of their car. He had switched his bike to the motor so it would be easier to climb a tall hill, though he stayed clear to the right of the road, near the shoulder. Jennifer and her entourage, who each held a can of beer, had been swerving continuously down the road and laughing about it. Jennifer was Officer D. Tish's niece, her parents had money, and she did not give a damn. Her carelessness was interpreted as courage, and she was considered fabulously cool. While Ryan was liked, Jennifer was, in a word, *admired.*

In the middle of a laugh, Jennifer hit Ryan with her car. It was violent, but he was not dead. The impact flung him over the car and into a ditch. Ryan lay there motionless, since his body was mangled, with one leg almost completely severed. But he was breathing. Jennifer, and those who had gone to school with him, left immediately. Though it was September, the night was creeping in, and it was chilly. Due to shock and massive blood loss, Ryan's body felt the cold all the more. It is not clear who, but someone made a call—maybe one of the kids in a moment of guilt, maybe someone who drove by. It does not much matter, because Ryan was nevertheless in that ditch for hours. Officer D. Tish was among the first responders.

Ryan was still breathing by the time they medevacked him to the hospital, though he was unconscious (it is difficult to say for how long he had been unconscious). Ryan's mother met him there, and held his ragged body. She was there for his final breaths. Her sobs came from deep within, or maybe deep below, drawn from a deep well that only those who have buried their children know of. It is said that, repeatedly, she spoke the word "why." A year later, she told people that she passed by the spot where Ryan had been hit, twice a day. And twice a day she wondered what he had been thinking before he was hit, and if he had felt any pain before he was unconscious.

Jennifer took her car, which had a smashed window, and dumped it in a lot with other junked cars. Her friends were very considerate of her needs, and helped her home. She did manage to tell her family, and they convinced her to turn herself in. Was it out of a sense of duty that they encouraged to do so, or was it confidence?—her uncle was Officer D. Tish, after all. It does not much matter, she still lied at the station. She said that someone had stolen her car, it was not her who had been driving. However, the police took a measurement of her blood alcohol level (which was twice the legal limit) and then arrested her anyway. But it did not much matter; though she was eventually found guilty of vehicular homicide, etc., she only received a four year sentence and was out on parole after two, which her family knew would happen. The irony is that this sentence was supposed to act as a "deterrent" to drunk driving, as the judge said, since he denied the first-offender waiver that would have dropped her jail time to 90 days. Community members, in their discussion of the tragedy to media, were quick to mention Ryan's DUI, and described what Jennifer had to face as "tough to bear" (her friends came out wholly unscathed and were hardly noted). And while Ryan had been the actual victim of a crime, the local newspaper spun the story in such a way that made it seem as though he was part of the problem.

Maybe the community Mark nostalgically pined after had been a façade all along, a place where the rich could get away with murder, as they can most anywhere. Indeed, Jennifer's wealth went way back—her family had once owned the majority of land where, by her day, a big resort had been built. And with all of the money now pouring into the island, those like Jennifer became reinvigorated by a newly formed net of bourgeois self-aggrandizement (which commanded extra respect from the lesser classes). Jennifer only spent two years thinking about what she did, and when she got out people were extraordinarily sympathetic to her experience. The so-called community seemed to talk about her as a victim as much or more than Ryan, who eventually became an afterthought of the past.

A handful of years prior to the dog-plague, when Mark was visiting the island, he overheard some gossip at a café. They murmured how sorry they felt for Jennifer and "those girls." And with a slightly disapproving tone, they added how Ryan's mother still was not "over it." Their voices had no true reason to be as hushed as they were, except for the weight of their own guilty subconscious. What they did not know was that Ryan's mother was, in fact, "over it"—for decades she had driven *over* that hill where he was struck. Twice a day, she was over it. Twice a day, she had a hill to climb.

∗∗∗

There is an old cliché that says you cannot step into the same river twice. But really, the whole world is like a river, and a certain place in this world is in a certain time that we know—in dreams, in childhood—it is not on a map.

MAGPIE

The crows were restless that day. They exhibited a behavior known officially as "cacophonous aggregation," usually occurring in the presence of a dead conspecific; when one or more crows gather around a fallen comrade and skold (a guttural squawk repeated in short concessions). These calls differ contextually from a simple alarm call to signal danger—the phenomenon is truly a crow funeral (of sorts), though the exact function of the behavior, and whether crows actually possess a complex understanding of death, is unknown. (How appropriate that a "murder of crows" can also be a funeral).

The crows were restless that day. They skolded and they skolded. They had circled the house since dawn; an incredible fluttering of wings, a great black mass, a ravenous, murderous, funeral of crows. One of their species had been shot by a high powered BB gun and lay dead on the cold lawn. The Butners kept their grass in immaculate condition—short, clean cut, perfect. The Butner family was relatively new to the neighborhood—Dan and Hannah Butner with their three boys: Richie, Billy, and Timmy. Richie, the oldest, was the spitting image of his father—indeed, he spat frequently, which served to emphasize his incessant strutting. It was an exact imitation of Dan's usual gait: a robotic yet cocky swagger that exuded his calculated control over things. Often this sense of control was produced through simple acts of destruction, most typically directed toward something "wild." These acts were usually unnecessary, but Dan could do them, so he did.

Dan had pruned back the lilacs that formed a natural fence with his neighbor. The flowers then became a shadow of their former glory, with sad sickly clumps appearing in dusty forgotten corners of the hedge. The resulting foliage was also nearly bare, forcing a view of Dan's obnoxiously large suburban home, which loomed over the other houses with an aggressively competitive tone. A large old spruce tree, which stood in the back corner of his yard, would sing year-round with its countless starling tenants—a mad cacophony that was both pleasant and jarring, like musicians in an orchestra pit tuning and practicing during intermission. Dan knocked the tree down, and laid a gravel patch for parking off the alley.

Dan had an untold number of vehicles, and frequently enlisted the labor of his sons to polish and vacuum them. The sounds of spring were soon replaced in the neighborhood by the constant drone of a vacuum. The sweet darkness of night, that one of his neighbors would often appreciate from his front porch (viewing the stars and moon) was replaced by several powerful strobe lights that wrapped around the entire Butner estate, shining effortlessly through the sparse branches of the lilacs.

And Dan mowed the lawn, he mowed obsessively, as if fighting a tireless battle against the stubborn green tide of life. Sometimes, Dan's mower would join in with the drone of the car-vacuum, needlessly idling engines, and the squeaks of waxing. Even the most suburbanite members of the neighborhood found the place to be stark and glaring. But Dan enjoyed that. He delighted in being disliked, as it gave him a feeling of power. His sons were learning to do this as well. Particularly Richie, who regarded this mode of being as one of life's great pleasures. In addition, the power of asserting oneself in this manner was a bonding experience for Richie, whose only other avenue was watching inspirational financial gurus on T.V. with his dad—that and, of course, his many imitations of his father; emulating him in many small details, even attempting to grow a little beard like Dan's.

Dan owned a big German shepherd. It was a good investment from a good breeder. It was an effective guard dog—big and potentially ferocious looking. It was also a very sensitive creature who would bark almost all day, expressing a morose and nervous loneliness. The poor beast lived in a small doghouse, in a small fenced-off area, separated from the rest of the yard, quarantined from the perfect lawn.

Timmy, the youngest, had what his parents described as a "complicated relationship" with the dog. He would put his face an inch from its muzzle, stretch his cheeks with his fingers, stick out his tongue, bulge his eyes, and make an unintelligible grinding "neh-neh-neh" utterance. When Timmy got in the mood, he would perform this stunt seemingly without end, usually as the dog was pushed up against the exterior wall near the front door. Timmy said he thought the dog looked "silly" when he did that—it would push down its snout, turn its ears back, and furrow its brow as if it were being reprimanded. Sometimes, however, the dog was not able to stand the assault, and so he would nip the air next to Timmy's head, letting out a pathetic yelp. Then Timmy would moan and cry performatively, seemingly without end, and call for his mom. He would yell "bad dog! baaad dooog!" and weakly push at the beast. The dog would then move away from Timmy, but the boy would follow and repeat. He would do this a few times, crying all the while, until his mother would step onto the front porch. His mother, Hannah, was as nondescript as a fast food menu, did not say much, and was never there. When she was at home, Timmy would engage in these desperate antics.

Billy could never screw his head on straight. It constantly tilted like a neglected scoop of ice cream on a cone. Sometimes, his lower lip sagged and his jaw drooped, as if the ice cream was dripping onto an apathetic fist. This effect on his lip and jaw, may have been caused by the lack of alignment, or because he enjoyed looking like that. Hannah did frequently attempt to screw his head on for him, but he wiggled so much that it would only worsen the placement of his cranium—he would go the rest of the day looking straight up at the sky, or down at his right shoulder, or down at his shoes. Once, Hannah's struggle to correct his noggin resulted in him facing directly backwards, yet sloped, so that he spent the whole day looking right at his ass.

Despite his head, the boy had tremendous aim—not so much with urination, and his parents forgave him for the mess in consideration of his condition (although, it is possible that Billy liked peeing *on* the toilet rather than *in*). But with a BB gun, he was a real sharpshooter. His favorite target was a bird, all birds, and he rarely missed. Any feathered creature found even remotely near the Butner's fence was toast. Billy was of course responsible for the crow that had been shot, causing the skolding commotion from the neighborhood crows, broadcasting their mourning with a warning, far and wide. It was the first crow Billy had shot, and it complimented his vast collection. The corpses of birds hid in the nooks and crannies of the suburban property, kicked there nonchalantly by Billy's family with subconscious efforts to place them out of sight, out of mind. Billy never cared to move the dead birds, not even by kicking. And so, the Butner's unwittingly kept an impressive graveyard—wrens, sparrows, finches, a downy woodpecker, turtle doves, countless starlings, two robins, and now this crow. The dead crow had not yet been shuffled to some shameless corner; it lay in the middle of the cold, sterile lawn, with early morning mist rising from the forgotten earth around it, like a weak sad spirit.

Billy always woke before the other Butners. It was a dark and furtive time for the boy—he would usually sneak into the kitchen and drink out of the milk jug. He was not supposed to do that, since it was not sanitary. But he liked that aspect of it. He would take big untidy swigs, letting a good portion of the milk that flowed into his mouth slop back out again. Much of this would trickle onto his chin, which he would lick and slurp with his abnormally large tongue. This action created a foam on his lips that would lather the rim of the jug once he took another drink. After getting his fill, he would take out his BB gun and load it—now was the time of the dawn chorus.

The skolds drew Billy to the open window of the upstairs landing. Sensing his menacing presence, the crows at once broke out into alarm, and then frantically flew away. Billy was disappointed to lose this golden opportunity to bag several more crows. But then something even more fortuitous occurred: on the edge of the roof-gutter there was perched a magpie.

"—Billy! Trash! Now!" came the untimely voice of his father.

It had been Billy's turn to dump the garbage into the bins at the back, which he forgot to do the night before. With loud thumping feet, he ran downstairs, grabbed the two heavy duty plastic bags in the kitchen (filled to the brim), and rushed to the alley. But alas, the garbage truck had already come and gone.

Yet, through some perverse serendipity, Billy noticed that the crew had accidently (or thoughtlessly) put the next door neighbor's recycle bin on the Butner's side. Billy seized the chance: he threw their rubbish into the neighbor's blue recycle bin. However, though it was a big bin, the garbage bags were so swollen with the fermenting pride of the Butner's refuse that they completely filled the thing. Billy knew then that the neighbor would simply react by taking the bags out, especially since there was no room left for him to put any of his recycling. So Billy took care to tear at the sides of the bags, making it difficult for the neighbor to remove them and expose Billy's deception to his parents. He was resourceful like that. Their used plastic gloves, dust masks, and tissues, slopped wantonly together with their copious food scraps: slimy heaps of rice, meatballs, noodles, corn chips, burger foils, candy bar wrappers, and so on. The frothy tumescent mixture steamed with the heat of decay and bubbled out of the tears Billy made, spilling forth into the neighbor's recycle bin like a lanced boil. Billy liked seeing that—but he also liked shooting birds, and he remembered the magpie.

Billy sprinted up the stairs in record time and snatched up his BB gun. (He had left the gun on the landing, resting on the floor though ready for action, and careless to anyone who might trip and set it off). To his amazement, the bird was still perched in the same location. Billy could no longer resist, he took aim and he shot... bullseye.

The magpie immediately dropped to the ground, stiff, redolent of a lifeless ornament that had just toppled over. Billy squeezed the barrel of his gun with sheer ecstasy. He clutched the piece close to his heart, basking in his sense of power and accomplishment, and then casually walked downstairs. Billy's muscles were warm with smug delight. His gait was light and fluffy, and he took his time.

He put on the shoes he had kicked off by the back door— one of the few rules of tidiness (such as throwing out the garbage) was removing your shoes. Billy rebelled by always flinging off his shoes, so that mud often splattered across the floor. His shoes were slip on rubber goloshes—he never learned to tie his shoes, though this was common in his day.

Billy checked for the bird corpse, but he could not find it. The magpie seemed to have fallen directly downward, but it was not there. He searched for several minutes, becoming more and more aware that the day was upon him and that the other Butners would soon rise. Dismayed, he returned indoors, and flicked off his laceless shoes from a standing position of slouched dejection. But then something stirred. One of his flung shoes managed to travel all the way to the kitchen and roll into something that lay on the floor. Billy became nervous, which was not like him. His teeth chattered cartoonishly and his blood ran cold. He held tightly onto his gun, ready to bludgeon with it, and crept slowly toward the movement.

As soon as Billy came close enough to see what it was, the heater came on—a loud thundering vent that blasted hot air with roaring ferocity. The sudden noise startled Billy and made his heart leap. The warmth rushing from the raging vent was so stifling he could barely think, as though he had been stunned.

A few days prior in science class, Billy had "learned" about some species of wasp that paralyze grasshoppers (so that they may lay eggs on the insect, which then hatch and feed on the living grasshopper—it has to be kept fresh for the little baby wasps). Billy had absorbed this information on one of the few occasions he had happened to listen to his teacher's lesson—in his day, listening was optional, and most kids brought devices to play with. It was called "divergent thinking." For just a moment, Billy feared that maybe he had been stung by such a wasp, which was why he stood inert— unable to defend himself against the hungry little mouths of hundreds of larvae.

Billy became aware again that he was holding his gun—a divine comfort that broke the wasp spell. He decided he would snap back into action. Billy used the gun to push the boot out of the way, with a sudden jerky maneuver.

Something moved in response and he jumped back, holding up his gun like a war club. But then his eyes focused and he finally saw what had been stirring: it was the magpie. The poor thing lay on its back and shifted between deathly stillness and undulating, almost unnatural, contortions. With its writhing came an oddly melodic, strangely sibilant, murmur. The vocalization sounded very much like it was trying to whisper something, but Billy could not make out what it was, if anything. Then Billy thought he heard it.

"Come here," it seemed to say, with a clear yet scratchy voice. There was a brief pause, which allowed Billy enough time to convince himself that the magpie had not actually said anything, it was his imagination forming words out of squawks and whistles. These were the sounds of it dying, Billy thought, and so relished in the pleasure of now observing the bird's suffering—usually they just dropped dead. But then it happened again. "Come here," it said, loud and unmistakable this time. Billy dropped the gun, intending to free up his mobility so that he could run upstairs in a panic. But again he was stunned and could not move. He just stood there, with his gun on the floor.

The magpie let out a long and torturous hiss as it slowly kicked its feet. This movement was repeated for a moment until, suddenly, its feet just seemed to vanish, perhaps sucked into its belly. The bird groaned horribly and shook its head from side to side. It began to convulse violently, its body flopping like a fish out of water. Then it stopped abruptly and was frozen.

Despite his fear and general immobility, Billy leaned in for a closer look, since he could scarcely believe his eyes: protruding out of the magpie's breast there was a toe, a pale human toe with a nail (well-clipped) and some hair on the knuckle. Moreover, it looked as though it was a right hallux (or "big toe") belonging to an adult man. The thing wriggled, as if it were feeling a cool lawn beneath it on a hot summer's day. The bird responded by quivering gently. Its eyes—that had so far been loosely present, though distant—rolled back into their sockets and became vacant. Still quivering (as dying beasts have done by the hands of humans for untold eons), the magpie opened its beak as wide as it could. Worming out of the bird's mouth came a right index finger, with a well-clipped nail (almost polished) and perfect skin.

Billy screamed. Other than the day he was born, he had never screamed before. And so, though it was not yet 6:00 AM, the entire household was immediately roused with fright. Billy's scream magically freed him from his inertia and he scampered upstairs like a bat out of Hell. He crammed himself under his parents' bedframe and moaned with fearful sobs. Hannah fell to the floor and attempted to console him. Billy's brothers stood in the doorway to their parents' bedroom, looking confused. Dan also looked confused, then leaned over to look at Billy and Hannah.

"What's going on?" Dan said.

A mist rose up the stairs to the second floor, billowing out from the kitchen area. Hannah was the first notice—"Dan! There's something here..."

Dan's jaw dropped, almost as low as Billy's jaw would lazily droop. His eyes widened. He grabbed his glasses by the nightstand and looked again.

"Dan! Do something!" Hannah said.

Dan did not exactly spring out of bed at her command. He moved at the same speed he always did. His slow and methodical swagger made him feel at ease—if you don't react calmly you'll lose control of the situation, he often told himself. Dan took his time putting on his slippers and snugly wrapping a thick robe around himself (despite his machismo, he liked wearing lots of layers, even in warm weather). While he got ready, Hannah squirmed in agitation and muttered something more to him, but he did not listen.

Dan wandered down the misty stairs with the same purpose as he would to fetch the morning paper (though in his day there were no morning papers). He walked toward the kitchen, where the thickest mist seemed to be. There, on the floor, was a pathetic lump of feathers, framed by a bare spot in the mist. Then Dan heard the door open behind him. He turned to look and thought he saw a pale naked man hastily exiting the house. Dan walked to the door to see if what he saw was real, but outside there was no sign of anybody, not even a stray cat—just the mist then, he thought. Billy must have left the door open, he thought.

The Butner's had a next door neighbor, named Max. He was about Dan's age. But Dan did not think Max was much of a man, and he would take whatever opportunity he could to talk down to Max—usually by speaking to him in a tone of suspicion or interrogation. Dan asked Max why he did not have Christmas lights, why he had not seen his wife and kid for a while (Max was going through a divorce), what Max did for a living (and if there was any money in it), what sort of education he had ("do you have your PhD, or just your Master's?"), and so on.

This neighbor, Max, was told by many that he needed to better himself. So his better self showed up one day, naked—he walked right in, put on Max's finest clothes, and then kicked him out. But before Max was completely out the door, his better self spit something out and put it in Max's hand: a round metal bead. Then he pushed Max down the steps of the front porch. Max did not put up much of a fight. He was tired. Besides, he needed to meet a friend for lunch, someone who was going to offer him advice about how to better himself. But Max's better self ran past him, having locked all the doors to the house, and hopped into the car.

"Natashia said she'd be there in ten minutes you idiot!" he said, and tore off.

Max was rarely late, but neither was he early. He stuck to the agreed time. However, in his day, people would frequently show up early, then send a brief message using their mobile phones saying that they were already there, usually with the simple text of "here." If you did not appear within a few minutes, you were seen as late. Being on time, in this way, became being late. Max spent as little time as he could on his phone, so he was always "late." His better self did not have this problem, and it was of course only a minor problem. But neither did his better self share the other problems, big or small.

Max guessed that maybe he could try and learn from his better self—he could wait for him to return home and then beg to be let back inside. But Max decided he would stay with his problems a bit longer, since he did not have any energy left to beg. Instead, he crawled through the bathroom window which had been left cracked open.

It was possible that his better self would come back with his wife, Joyce, and their young daughter Deirdre. He loved Deirdre, but he would have to live in the closet and wait for his chance to reintegrate, if he was lucky. And maybe his better self would never leave. Max would have to live off food scraps and sleep on a pile of dirty laundry… He thought he should just go, but he did not know where to go.

THE LITTLE SHADOW

The crows were restless that day. They exhibited a behavior known officially as "cacophonous aggregation," usually occurring in the presence of a dead conspecific; when one or more crows gather around a fallen comrade and skold (a guttural squawk repeated in short concessions). These calls differ contextually from a simple alarm call to signal danger – the phenomenon is truly a crow funeral (of sorts), though the exact function of the behavior, and whether crows actually possess a complex understanding of death, is unknown. (How appropriate that a "murder of crows" can also be a funeral).

The crows were restless that day. They skolded and they skolded. They had circled the house since dawn; an incredible fluttering of wings, a great black mass, a ravenous, murderous funeral of crows. One of their species lay dead near the house. No one was home, no one had been home for some time, nor does this narration possess any further knowledge on the subject—the creature's death, therefore, remains unaccountable. The house was in a condemned neighborhood. It was a time of plague. Skolds rang louder than ever before, uninterrupted by the otherwise incessant hum of lawnmowers, weedwhackers, passing trucks, and various idle engines.

The sun was high, prime conditions for shadows. A little shadow stood outside, sheltered by the exposure of a vacant street— it had lost its body. After having wandered for what seemed like ages (or maybe only moments), the shadow recognized the house and suspected its body was within. However, a thick shade permeated the house's insides. It was heavy and swollen with darkness, as if the dark could hardly be contained. Therefore, the shadow could not enter, for it would be swallowed up by the hungry dark.

On the road, the coming night could also consume the shadow, though it would be regurgitated by morning. It was where light could not penetrate that sought to steal the shadow for good. The shadow wondered if the dark house was made that way by some insatiable ingestion of other shadows, whose fate were to melt into a tumescent stomach of architecture. The shadow approached for a closer look and thought it heard the groan of countless shadows, mulched into one agonizing howl. Did they know they were they?

It sat on the light stained walkway. The warmth seemed to betray its interior. Leaves on a quaking aspen began to quiver in the breeze, causing dappled shade to flicker near the front door. The shadow moved itself there, becoming soaked in the cold leafy shade, like a gentle rain. Without its body it had no true tears, and so it borrowed the leafy soft repose for its sorrowful expression.

The shadow looked at the walkway and saw its simulated weeping for what it was. More and more it realized its flatness, stretching out on empty surfaces, without substance. It was becoming aware that it did not step firmly, like most people, nor like any living thing. The ground could rumble under their feet and shake with their emphatic stomps. Rather, the shadow slipped along quietly, and lighter than light—indeed, built from the absence of light. There is a light in people, illuminating every aspect of their being—to look at someone is to see light. But this shadow had never felt light in its own form, without its body. Really, it did not even know its own form, it asked itself if it was nothing.

The streets were empty. In empty places, such as these, there is a silence that yet stirs, a rustling wrestle with the wind, exuding a profound isolation, and a profound indifference. Did it matter if the shadow was or was not? Maybe, and maybe that is why the shadow was so afraid of darkness, of being consumed by its own nothing. By contrast, the house had form, great imposing form. It seemed to have a life of its own. It seemed to thrive on occupying space, smug like a full belly. Nevertheless, the house was normal, a spacious tract home like many on that block—though the house seemed to be the origin of all the others.

The shadow lay prostrate before the monolith to normalcy, expecting the proximity to its body inside to evince some sense of humanity. The shadow entertained the fantasy of human strength blowing through the front door and infusing itself into the shadow, expanding like a balloon. The shadow dreamed of peeling off the concrete ground and out of flatness forever. It imagined taking its inflated self into the belly of the house, without fear, embracing its body with love and carrying it away. There was a field that span out in a westward direction, past two old playgrounds surrounded by caution tape shivering in the breeze (back behind the housing development, behind the cream-colored fences). The shadow pictured carrying its body there, to wander distantly without care.

With that the shadow noticed a sickly sallow sunbeam. The string of light was shining, somehow, into the house's interior abyss through a window. The shadow inched near to the little sunbeam and contemplated. This was its opening, though it was razor thin. The sun began to hang low, now was the shadow's chance, now or never...

No, never then. It is impossible, the shadow thought. Without voice for its body to hear, it gestured what shadows mean when they say "sorry." And so, keeping to its flat confines, the shadow slithered between the playgrounds to the field alone, to meld with darkness and become a feast for nocturnal creatures. The grass and weeds seemed to usher the shadow with a persistent "shhh" in the wind.